MW00917503

An Adventurous Airport story by Cleous "GloWry" Young

Copyright © 2020 Cleous G. Young

www.theairportadventure.com

Edited by:	**Rita Hubbard**
Illustrated by:	**Melani Alarcon**
Contributed Suitcase Artwork by:	**Odane Skervin,** *upcoming artist*
ASIN:	**B08M8GW25Y**

A special 'THANKS' to my dearly beloved Grandmother.
The ROCK of my childhood's growth and development.
Mrs. Hortense Nelson (Cookie)

MI CASA, ES SU CASA
BEST FRIEND SERVICE
B F S

To: Emilio and Daniela

Thank you for what you have done and continue to do in helping individuals share their stories with the world. You are the jet bridge that covers the gap to allow so many to transition to the airplane of their life, which gave them the opportu... to take off. May this Book-A-Zine enrich your thoughts and help you to continue to do wha... you do best. May a million authors come to the hands of your service. May their appetite be satisfied and their thoughts be fulfill... with good merits. May your family continue to be safe and reach higher heights in your busines... LIVE SAFELY!

C Young

9/4/2021

Be Safe! Stay Healthy! Build New Possibilities!

How the Series Began

> *I was unsafe around friends that I should have been safe around... and when I found out how unsafe I was, I realized that my mentality was also in turbulence...*

All my life, I believed I had friends that I could trust. But one day, some of those friends proved me dead wrong. I felt unsafe as if a rug was snatched from underneath my feet. My mind was in a state of turbulence. As I worked through my uneasiness, a strange revelation came to me about an airplane's Black Box. I suddenly realized that I needed a Black Box moment as a coping mechanism. I created a Black Box Friendship (BBF), where a special friend of mine allowed me to safely share my most pressing thoughts of what caused turbulence in my mentality. It worked! I was back to my usual self of eating correctly, sleeping well at night, and concentrating on the tasks at hand. I also began to search for other ways that the airport industry (one of the safest industries out there) can help people who are feeling unsafe and want to recover from their most challenging circumstances. What I discovered was an untapped goldmine that the global community needs. Thus, the creation of The Airport Adventure Book-A-Zine Series.

How to Scan a QR Code?

1. Download and Open a QR code reader on your smartphone or compatible device.

2. Hold your phone or device over the QR code so that it's clearly visible within your device's screen.

3. The video will open for you to enjoy!

Table of CONTENTS

BOOK

Book's Dedication

Thank you to those who have contributed toward making this book project a reality, especially in the field of endorsements. I genuinely appreciate every effort. The book, in the high regard, is dedicated to Clinton Lewis, whose selfless commitment, dedication, prayers, financial contributions, reliability, unyielding resources, positive support and loyalty to the author helped make this project a reality.

Innovating a project or concept takes an exceptional courage of its own. It is a good feeling knowing that there is a person in your corner that you can always rely on to pull the process through no matter what. It is what I would call 'destination safety', which is the support and reliability that makes sure that you get to your destination. We all need a destination safety support and Black Box Friendship around us at some point in our life, which will help to carry the weight of what it takes to reach a destination. Thank you, Clinton Lewis, for always being there and for your encouraging support throughout the project.

How to use this Book-A-Zine

(First, what is a Book-A-Zine and how it came about?)

A Book-A-Zine is the blending of a picture book with a magazine. The concept came to me after working as a 4th-grade teacher. I noticed that the school always ordered books and magazines for supplemental learning. These materials were in separate formats, so they were ordered separately.

Having such understanding after the Black Box experience, I got the idea to blend them and create an innovative children's book: A Book-A-Zine. The storybook would entertain like the typical children's book, but it would get added support from the magazine details at the end. The magazine details are a good fit for resolving the many complaints that students learn in the academic field but remain illiterate in the realities of life. With a Book-A-Zine, students have an alternate way of learning academics while connecting socially and realistically.

How to use this book:

01 This series follows the adventures of the Kite family. The current members are Mom (Mrs. Tee) and Dad (Mr. Pluss), Ribbit, Flyy, Good Samaritan, Security Guard, Prospect, Driver, Gate Agent, Face Watch, and Rocko.

Each adventure focuses on personal and social safety. **02**

03 Each adventure is shared by a NARRATOR, who helps readers understand what is going on in the story and what they will learn from the adventure.

Each story contains **SAFETY INFO ALERTS** (safety information alerts) that come through conversations in the story or information shared by the narrator. We may not be aware of these safety hints in our everyday lives, but they are useful in increasing safety as well as socialization skills. Readers are encouraged (via the narrator) to watch for the safety info alerts in each chapter. **04**

05 Each story includes **boldly highlighted** vocabulary words that will help the reader understand the Magazine section of the book.

Each adventure has an end-of-chapter activity. **06**

07 Each adventure is written like a theatrical script, which offers a different reading format from the usual paragraph style of children's storybooks. Therefore, each adventure can be read individually, as a class, or students can act it out in a school theater.

Introduction to the Story:

Before you begin your Book-A-Zine Adventure, let's take a short time to prep you for what you are about to engage in. The Airport Adventure 'LiVe Safely' is the first story of the Book-A-Zine series that will take readers/discoverers on a world of adventures. There are four main characters that are different from the other characters in this picture book. They are the Kite Family: a mother and father, and two young children, Ribbit and Flyy.

In the opening pages, Ribbit & Flyy, are on their way to the airport for their trip to spend time with their grandparents for the summer. Ribbit and Flyy are little discoverers who like to discover new things. This first adventure begins in the Philadelphia International Airport, also known as PHL (Airport code).

By the way, Ribbit and Flyy, love technology and social media, especially live streaming, so they will be sharing their adventure live. As the adventure unfolds, readers get to interact and experience the action as well. So, buckle up! It's going to be an adventurous ride.

SPECIAL NOTE:

The author used Kite characters because the kite is a method of aviation: In fact, it was once the first line of aviation possibilities. The kite is an easy way to connect aviation and safety principles with children. But more importantly, it is a way to show how something as simple as a kite brought forth new possibilities of us flying on a commercial aircraft today. With this in mind, how can your simple idea bring new possibilities in the future? Enjoy the adventure. So long till we meet again.

Be Safe!

A Little Note About Safety:

The airport industry is able to achieve such a high level of safety because SAFETY is their priority, and thus they create the space for it to exist. According to Alexandre de Juniac, IATA's Director General and CEO, "**4.3 billion passengers flew safely on 46.1 million flights in 2018**." The airport sees the value in investing short and longer visions around having passengers reach their destinations safely. The same can happen if we take a look at short and long-term investments in prioritizing SAFETY for Human Socialization. We would have an astounding future; a future of humans safely navigating amongst each other from one destination to another, and from old realities to new possibilities. Welcome to the first installment of The Airport Adventure: LiVe Safely.

Safety is paramount, so pay close attention!

CHAPTER - 01

M.P.

AT HOME

■ **RIBBIT:**

"Hi, my name is Ribbit, but you can call me RBT for short. I am a huge fan of superheroes. My favorite superhero is Captain America: red, white, and blue."

■ **FLYY:**

"And my name is Flyy. They call me that because I dress real fly. I like to dress up, so I added the extra letter 'y' to dress up my name. Welcome to our home and our 'Adventurous Airport story.' How are you doing today?"

■ **RIBBIT:**

"We hope you're having a safe day today. If not, after this story is finished, we hope you will feel safe and much better. We are so excited about this trip because it's our first trip to visit Grandma and Grandpa. Best of all, we get to go to a beach that has lots of sun and a cool breeze that tickles your skin. We anticipate getting there safe and sound, so please help us to spot the SAFETY INFO ALERTS as we go along. Thank you in advance for your participation."

THE TWO HIGH FIVE EACH OTHER.

■ **FLYY:**

"Today, you'll get to come along with us. When you do, it will be like you are live on a Facebook or Instagram stream. It is what we call the Book-A-Zine Live. Except for the time that we go through TSA security, you will see or hear everything we encounter at the airport in the moment we encounter them. Safety is an essential part of our adventure. Why? Because we will be entering the airport and safety is a vital component of its daily operation. So, whatever is important to someone or something, is what we will encounter when we interact with that person or thing! So, come along, and if you see something unsafe, be sure to let us know. Remember, we anticipate getting there safe and sound."

■ RIBBIT:

"First, you must understand that we are too young to GO to the airport by ourselves. Going alone would be an unsafe thing for us to do. We can eat by ourselves, tie our shoelaces by ourselves, and bike by ourselves, but we can't go to the airport by ourselves. So, guess who will take us?"

■ FLYY:

"Our P-A-R-E-N-T-S. That's right, our parents! So, buckle-up, and let's GO for the adventure."

THEY SAFELY RUN TO THE CAR.

■ RIBBIT:

"Mom! Dad! We are all set and ready to GO!"

■ FLYY:

"That was our first SAFETY INFO ALERT. Did you catch it? Notice that our first form of safety is **communication**. By **communicating** and letting our parents know that we are ready, we are also letting them know what to do as well. This way, we will all have a mutual understanding of what is going on. We must all learn how to **communicate** with our parents effectively, and our parents must learn to **communicate** with us effectively. That's our first SAFETY INFO ALERT. It is unsafe when parents and children do not communicate effectively with each other."

MOM AND DAD COMES OUT WITH THE SUITCASES.

■ NARRATOR:

"And so, the parents pack the suitcases in the car and find their respective seats. Dad is the driver, Mom is the front seat navigator, and RBT and Flyy are the backseat passengers. Soon they will be dropped off at the airport as 'unaccompanied minors,' but not before their parents watch them take off in the airplane."

■ **FLY Y:**

"Do you know what an 'unaccompanied minor' is?"

■ **RIBBIT:**

"If you don't know, an 'unaccompanied minor' is a child between the ages of five and fourteen who flies with the assistance of a flight attendant because his or her parent is not available to accompany him or her. For safety reasons, the child must be dropped off or picked up by a trustworthy relative. Children ages fifteen to seventeen are considered unaccompanied minors as well; however, they can travel on their own without the assistance of a flight attendant."

■ **FLYY:**

"Parents or guardians take advantage of this service offered by the airlines all the time when they want to send their children to visit other family members or friends, but they are unable to GO with their children. **So if you are…**"

■ **RIBBIT:**

"Hey Flyy! Fasten your seatbelt. It's time to GO. By the way, children, did you spot the two **SAFETY INFO ALERTS** we just gave you? We will provide the answers at the end of this chapter. In the meantime, you may want to re-read to see if you noticed them."

■ **FLYY:**

"Thank you for reminding me, RBT. That was a **KIND** thing to do. We should buckle our seatbelt when we are traveling in the back of a vehicle, especially when we are a minor. As I was saying earlier, if you are between the ages of five and fourteen, you are considered an 'unaccompanied minor' by the airline industry."

■ **NARRATOR:**

"All aboard! As Dad is pulling out of the driveway, he makes a sudden stop. His cellphone is ringing, and he answers it. It's his job. There is an emergency, and they need him to come in right away. He is a doctor, and sometimes doctors are on call. Dad safely communicates the details of the emergency to his family.

Meanwhile, Mom takes over, and Dad steps out of the vehicle so he can stay behind and go to the hospital. Even though they are a family, each of the four family members sometimes have their own **INDIVIDUAL** role to play. Did you spot the SAFETY INFO ALERT? First, Dad stopped the vehicle to take the phone call. That was a **KIND** thing for him to do for his family. Otherwise, he risked being in an accident while driving and taking an emergency call --- which is a little different from a regular phone call."

■ RIBBIT:

"That's how life is sometimes. A planned adventure can be interrupted by an emergency. You just have to learn how to navigate around the emergency if it is not too critical, just like Dad did. On the other hand, let's keep rolling."

■ NARRATOR:

"Mom takes over, and they continue their journey to the airport."

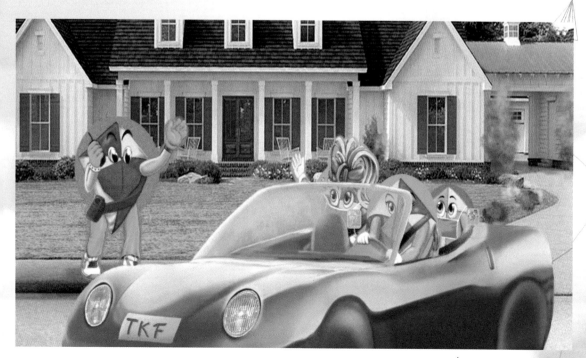

Safety Info Alert Answers:

1. **On page 20,** RBT interrupted the conversation as he alerted Flyy to put on her seatbelt. Interrupting someone without using manners may put that person in an unsafe position because the person is not able to say what he or she intended to. So, if you interrupt someone while the person is speaking, remember to go back and allow the person to finish what he or she meant to say. Example: Water is intended to flow through a hose. If you block the water from flowing, it eventually builds up and may later cause the hose to expand and break. The same applies when a person (made up of at least 70% water) is interrupted and not allowed to speak what he or she intended to.

2. **On page 20,** RBT also alerted Flyy to put on her seatbelt. Buckling your seatbelt is a safety precaution that is required while traveling in the seat of a vehicle or on an aircraft during takeoff, turbulence, and landing. It is not only the law to wear your seatbelt; it is the SAFE thing to do because it may prevent injury if the vehicle or aircraft you are riding in, is in an accident.

Vocabulary Words:

The two vocabulary words are **KIND** and **INDIVIDUAL**. Write their definition.

KIND —————————————————————

INDIVIDUAL —————————————————

CHAPTER - 02

S.G.

CHECKING IN

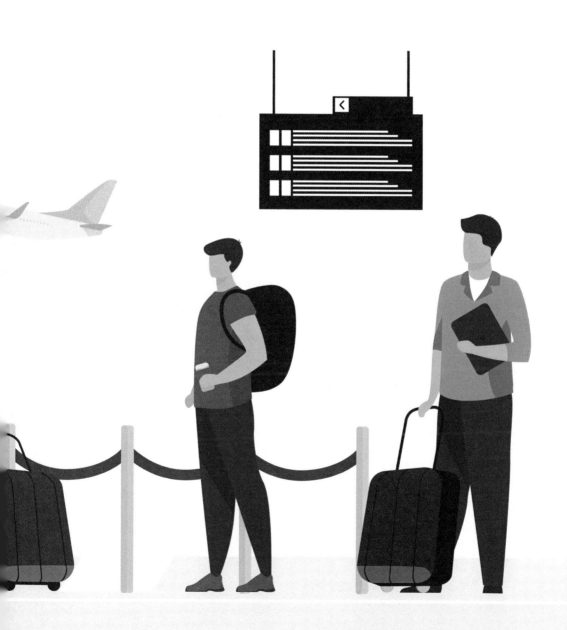

■ **NARRATOR:**

"RBT, Flyy, and Mom make it to the airport SAFELY. However, it isn't long before Dad calls to check up on them to make sure their adventure is still in progress, and his **TEAM** is safe. His call comes right on time, just before the check-in. Did you notice the **SAFETY INFO ALERT** that Dad just carried out? It is always good to call and follow up after an emergency to make sure everything is running as smoothly as it was before the emergency. Kudos to Dad for being a team player, even while he is away.

Because the children are 'unaccompanied minors,' Mom will assist them through the boarding process of the airplane. She will have to wait until the aircraft takes off on the runway before she can leave. Dad wants to make sure that they safely do so, so he calls to check-in.

Meanwhile, all the needed paperwork is checked and verified by the ticket agent. It allows them to GO to the next step, TSA."

■ **RIBBIT:**

"Do you know what the letters TSA means?"

■ **FLYY:**

"I will help you if you don't know. It means Transportation Security Administration. It is called TSA for short. The TSA is an agency of the U.S. Homeland Security that oversees the public as they travel in and out of the United States. An emergency like 9/11, when an airplane crashed into the Twin Towers in New York, and another airplane crashed into the Pentagon in Washington, D.C., called for more security at the airport. This call is similar to how Mom was called upon after Dad had an emergency. That is how the need for a lot more security at airports across the country was called on after the 9/11 emergency."

▪ RIBBIT:

"It is all about traveling SAFELY. Who doesn't want to travel to their destination safely? That's why we have agencies like the TSA. But they are not the only ones that should make your travel safe. Safety starts with YOU! Again, safety starts with YOU.

It is also the responsibility of everyone that works at the airport to make sure the passengers' journey is safe and comfortable."

▪ FLYY:

"There is an airport safety motto. Do you know it? It goes like this: 'If you see something, say something.' Anyone can say something if they see something suspicious. Do you see anything suspicious in the picture on page 27?"

▪ MOM:

"It's time to get off live stream now, guys."

▪ RIBBIT:

"Thanks, Mom. But before I do, I will ask: Did you find the suspicious backpack tucked away on the counter? That is a **SAFETY INFO ALERT**. You never know what dangerous products could be in the backpack that may cause harm to all of us. See you on the other side."

HANGS UP LIVE STREAM...

■ **NARRATOR:**

"Why do you think Flyy and RBT had to check-in at the front even though they had already purchased tickets? Think about being in a classroom as the teacher takes attendance. Taking attendance lets the school staff know who is present and who is absent on the day attendance is taken. It is one of the reasons airline passengers have to check-in. It lets specific airport staff know who is present and who is absent. Also, if a passenger requires a wheelchair or other special assistance, checking in allows specific airport staff to begin preparing the wheelchair or additional special assistance to accommodate the passenger. So, checking in and having the right credentials is very important. It is also a SAFETY protocol.

It helps to identify who has a ticket to fly on the airplane, and it also helps to assure that the name on the ticket belongs to the person who is checking in on the flight. Mom, RBT, and Flyy are about to go through TSA. Go ahead and complete the vocabulary activity. They will see you on the other side."

Vocabulary Word: ─────────────────────────

The vocabulary word is **TEAM**. Write the definition.

CHAPTER — 03

TSA CHECK POINT

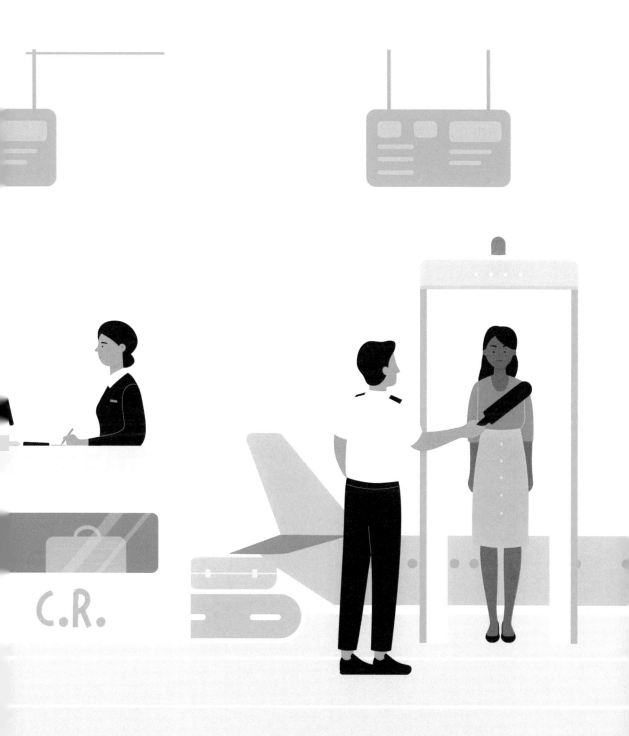

C.R.

NARRATOR:

"All three go through the TSA checkpoint line, even though Mom isn't flying with them. Mom has received a temporary pass at the check-in desk that allows her to follow RBT and Flyy to board the airplane. All three must remove their footwear, metal jewelry, and any pocket items that may set off the alarm scanner at the TSA checkpoint. The TSA staff also asks travelers to remove belts as well, but since they aren't wearing belts, they are good to GO. It is all based on SAFETY regulations, and those who have no metals, belts, or other unsafe goods that seem dangerous are allowed to pass through smoothly. Anyone wearing metals, carrying weapons, or transporting dangerous goods will set off the alarm. If this is YOU, a TSA officer will stop you and check your belongings. Guess who made it through safely and smoothly? All three!"

FLYY:

"That was a quick check. I guess we didn't have any weapons, belts, metals, or dangerous goods on us."

RIBBIT:

"Readers, do you know what dangerous goods are?"

FLYY:

"I'll tell them. They are items that are unsafe to carry on the airplane because they can cause an explosion or fire, or can be used as a weapon to harm others. The Federal Aviation Administration, also known as the FAA, will fine an airline up to $80,000 per occurrence for violating the policy of the dangerous goods. This violation happens when an airline does not check its passengers accurately and ultimately allows a passenger to travel with unsafe goods. Various airport employees are trained to identify dangerous goods, so if they ask you if you are traveling with any, don't feel they are being nosey or are invading your privacy. They are asking as a precaution. They just want to make sure that everyone makes it safely to their destination, and it also makes the airport run safely and smoothly."

■ RIBBIT:

"Do you need some examples of dangerous goods? Here are a few: lithium batteries or devices with lithium batteries; aerosol spray cans; electronic cigarettes; hoverboards; explosives; alcohol beverages over 70% proof; flammable solids or liquids; defense sprays like tear gas, mace, pepper spray; and marijuana. In case you are wondering how a small child like me knows all these things, guess what? Our parents made us go to the airline's website and read the Do's and Don'ts so we would comply, especially since we are unaccompanied minors. I wanted to bring my hoverboard on the trip, and that is how we found out it was included on the list of the unsafe, dangerous goods to travel with on the airplane. So, no hoverboard for me! But I know it's for my own safety and the safety of others. Did you spot the **SAFETY INFO ALERT** in what we just discussed? Complying, when flying, is a safe thing to do for yourself and for others that are flying as well. Remember this poetic message, complying, when flying is a safe thing to do, for others and YOU."

■ FLYY:

"I **ENCOURAGE** you to do the same thing before you travel. Remember, safety starts with YOU. With your parent's assistance, go on the airline's website and see which items you can travel with and which you cannot, especially in this pandemic. Reading the details on the airline's website is what helped me to understand that my suitcase is limited to 50 lbs. It is a part of the airplane's weight and balance restrictions. You see, having too much or too little weight on the aircraft while it is in flight mode, is unsafe and can cause an accident. Safety is also knowing what to do and knowing when to do it can also make you safe."

■ RIBBIT:

"Imagine if every passenger snuck suitcases that are too heavy onto the airplane, and no one noticed. Then, imagine that the airplane suddenly starts to go down while in flight mode because it cannot handle the extra weight. It could lead to a severe and even fatal plane crash, and all because the passengers didn't follow the weight restrictions.

The airport staff is not trying to prevent passengers from traveling with a lot of items. It's about the SAFETY of the airplane while it is in flight mode."

■ FLYY:

"It is all a part of us preparing for our adventure. The more prepared we are for our adventure, the safer our adventure will be. That is a **SAFETY INFO ALERT** for you. In other words, be prepared, even though you cannot always prevent emergencies."

■ NARRATOR:

"So, with no metals, weapons, or dangerous goods, the three went through the TSA check point smoothly. That's a security process for all airports. Sorry, you were not able to see the process through the live stream. They will now turn back on their live stream. See you soon."

Vocabulary Word:

The vocabulary word is **ENCOURAGE**. Write down the definition.

CHAPTER – 04

THE UNSAFE DECISION

NARRATOR:

"RBT decides to make a bathroom pit stop, but not before his Mom prompts him about being on the live stream."

MOM:

"Remember to turn off your live stream."

RIBBIT:

"Oh yeah, I almost forgot."

FLYY:

"Did you catch that **SAFETY INFO ALERT**? RBT was about to enter the bathroom, but it is inappropriate and unsafe to videotape or show a minor using the bathroom."

RIBBIT TEMPORARILY SHUTS OFF HIS WATCH'S LIVE STREAM.

NARRATOR:

"RBT returns from the bathroom, and then he, Mom, and Flyy walk towards Gate F33, which is their departure gate. It is quite a distance from gate F1, but they make it safely. They check in with the Gate Agent and take their seats close to the front of the boarding area. Mom and Flyy are comfortable, but not RBT. While Mom reads her favorite magazine and Flyy talks on her phone, RBT begins to fidget. It's his first time flying, and he is trying to pretend he is not nervous, but he can't. Nature takes over, and before he knows it, it's time to use the bathroom once again."

RIBBIT:

"Mom, I have to go to the bathroom."

MOM:

"Can it wait? You will board in a few minutes, and you can use the bathroom on the airplane."

RIBBIT:

"I have to go really bad!"

HE SQUEEZES HIS LEGS TOGETHER.

NARRATOR:

"Mom looks at the boarding time and all the people are now standing around her. She doesn't want to give up her upfront seating position."

MOM:

"Flyy. Flyy!"

FLYY:

"Oh, yes Mom!"

MOM:

"Do you remember the last bathroom that we just walked past?"

FLYY:

"Yes Mom."

MOM:

"Can you take your brother? He needs to go badly. I don't want to lose this seat in front of the gate agent and miss your chance of boarding on time."

FLYY:

"Sure."

NARRATOR:

"RBT and Flyy walk quickly and safely to the bathroom. It is very **KIND** of Flyy to agree to take her little brother to the bathroom. They walk past a suitcase without noticing it. RBT really has to go. The first bathroom, which is the closest, has a long line of people that stretches outside. The second bathroom is the same. Flyy starts to feel the urge to use the bathroom as well. The siblings finally arrive at the third bathroom. Flyy looks at the line to the women's restroom and sees that it is even longer than the men's line. Did you catch the SAFETY INFO ALERTS? The first alert is the suitcase that is lying around by itself. The second alert is that the siblings have walked to a bathroom that is further away than expected without communicating it to their mother. Flyy tells RBT what he should do."

FLYY:

"Listen, when you are finish using the bathroom, stand over there to the side and wait for me."

RIBBIT:

"Copy that!"

■ **NARRATOR:**

"Five minutes pass and RBT is patiently waiting where he was told to wait. But on the seventh-minute mark, he notices an adorable puppy running toward him, and a group of people chasing and shouting, "Rocko! Rocko! Stop him! Stop him!" But Rocko is yards ahead of them. RBT sees this as an easy stop and a way for him to become an airport superhero. He plans to transition from a nervous child who had to go the bathroom to the airport superhero who catches the adorable puppy, <u>a role he never got the opportunity to be at home, especially since his sister always outshines him.</u> It is also a **KIND** thing to do for someone else who is in distress.

So, with these thoughts quickly running through his mind, RBT braces himself forward and kneels with open arms that welcome Rocko. But Rocko has different plans. The first plan is not to be captured, and the next plan is to keep on running. Like the little cow that jumped over the moon, Rocko leaps over RBT and keeps going.

Poor RBT thinks he has him, but… he doesn't. He turns quickly and watches Rocko stop at a distance and look back at him. Then RBT turns and looks at the gap between himself and the group of people chasing Rocko. 'I can still be a superhero since my sister is not around,' he thinks, as he runs toward Rocko. Rocko, on the other hand, runs even further away.

There is an escalator ahead in the distance, and that's where Rocko decides to run. He stands there, panting at the top of the escalator and looking at poor RBT who mounts the steps one by one. Rocko playfully barks, and RBT takes it as a hint to continue. 'I can be the superhero if I can get to the top of the steps,' he says to himself.

As RBT gets closer to the top of the escalator, Rocko moves backward. Finally, RBT makes it to the top and faces Rocko. Rocko looks at RBT, and RBT looks at Rocko, whose great moment of escape has come to an end. RBT gets his breathing under control from running up the steps, and thinks to himself, 'It's over now.'

Remembering how swift Rocko is, RBT puts more effort into capturing him than he did earlier. "Not so fast," he cries as he half-leaps ahead like a frog, determined to catch Rocko. But Rocko quickly moves out the way.

RBT rolls into the direction of the doors. Lucky for him, the doors have a motion sensor and open automatically. Otherwise, he would have jammed himself into the doors and with such a forceful leap, he would surely have been hurt. He jumps up, brushes himself off, and then tries to get back through the open doors. It is too late! The doors close automatically and all RBT sees is a red sign that says, **DO NOT ENTER**. He bangs on the door, but no one except Rocko can hear him. The banging scares Rocko and he runs back down the escalator just in time to meet up with the group that had been chasing him.

Rocko's owner is overwhelmed and hugs him passionately. The celebration of the group's reunion with Rocko makes them forget that someone had been chasing him. Therefore, there is no need to go up the escalator, which means there is no way for anyone to hear RBT knocking. This means there is no way for him to get back inside, which means that he will miss his flight unless someone is able to rescue him. Poor RBT! He wanted to be a superhero, but now he is at ground zero!"

Open-Ended Activity:

Can you identify the vocabulary word in this chapter? Write it down and also write why you think this word keeps repeating in different chapters?

CHAPTER – 05

D.G.

THE RECOVERY

"Flyy finally exits the bathroom. She begins to look for RBT in the place where she told him to wait, but he is not there. She sees a group of people walking past with a puppy, but RBT is not there, either. She walks to the men's bathroom and calls him from the outside, but there is no answer.

She politely asks a gentleman to check the bathroom to see if there is a young boy inside one of the stalls, but no luck! Suddenly, Flyy begins to panic. "Has someone kidnapped my only brother?" she thought to herself.

Even though it was for a good cause, Flyy did not follow the safety protocol her parents taught her. Flyy and RBT are unaccompanied minors, so their parents have warned them about stranger-danger, and how they should not talk to strangers. Yet, Flyy breaks this rule when she asked the stranger to check the bathroom stalls.

What if this was a hint for him to take advantage of her situation? Did you notice the **SAFETY INFO ALERT**? In a case like this, you should look for a person in uniform, someone who has on a name badge or lanyard ID. Someone with these credentials would more easily be recognized as a safer person than a stranger without any form of uniform, name badge, or lanyard ID. Take that as a safety hint when you are out in public and need to ask for help. Remember, safety starts with YOU.

In the meantime, Flyy walks over next to the wall and sobs over the loss of her little brother. A Good Samaritan passenger sees her as she shrivels up against the wall. The **KIND** thing to do is to check on her, and that is just what the Good Samaritan does."

GOOD SAMARITAN:

"What's wrong?"

FLYY:

"Someone might have kidnapped my little brother."

GOOD SAMARITAN:

"What? Are you sure?"

FLYY:

"I don't know. I told him to wait for me right here while I used the bathroom. I came out and he's not here."

GOOD SAMARITAN:

"Did you check in the bathroom to see if he is still in there?"

NARRATOR:

"Flyy nods her head and continues to sob."

GOOD SAMARITAN:

"You know what? I just walked past a security guard around the corner. Let's see if he can help us find your little brother."

NARRATOR:

"Flyy gets up off the floor with the help of the Good Samaritan. They walk around the corner to see the security guard. The Good Samaritan approaches him calmly."

GOOD SAMARITAN:

"Hi. I saw this young lady crying on the floor and she said that someone might have kidnapped her little brother."

■ SECURITY GUARD:

| "Is that true young lady?"

■ FLYY:

| "I think so. I told him to wait for me after he used the bathroom. When I came out, he wasn't there."

■ SECURITY GUARD:

| "What's your name?"

■ FLYY:

| "Flyy."

■ SECURITY GUARD:

| "What's your brother's name?"

■ FLYY:

| "Ribbit. But people call him RBT."

■ SECURITY GUARD:

| "How old is he?"

■ FLYY:

| "7."

■ **SECURITY GUARD:**

| "And you?"

■ **FLYY:**

| "14."

■ **SECURITY GUARD:**

| "Oh, so you are both unaccompanied minors. Where is your parent or guardian?"

■ **FLYY:**

| "My mom is at Gate F33."

■ **SECURITY GUARD:**

| "Wow! That's a long way away from here. What does your brother look like and have you alerted your mom?"

■ **FLYY:**

| "He looks like..."

■ **NARRATOR:**

| "Before she begins the description, her Face Watch beeps in for a video call. It's RBT!"

■ **FLYY:**

| "Oh, my goodness! He's alive. Hello, hello?"

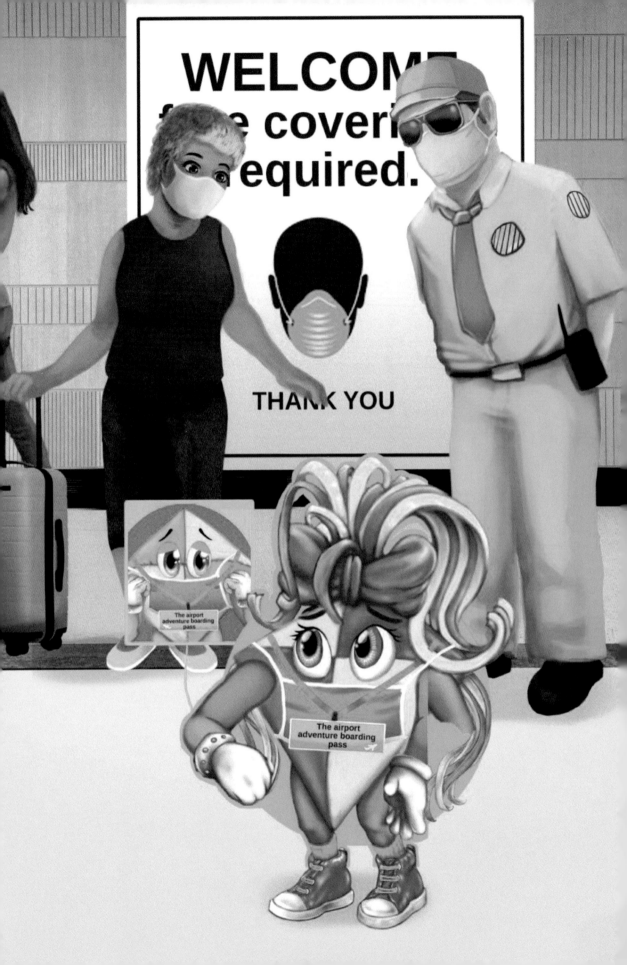

RIBBIT:

"Hey! I'm locked out!"

FLYY:

"Locked out of what?"

RIBBIT:

"Outside. I don't know. The door has a red sign that says, **DO NOT ENTER!**"

FLYY:

"Where are you?"

RIBBIT:

"I don't' know. I was chasing a puppy; it came upstairs and I got locked out."

FLYY:

"What puppy? What upstairs? Didn't I tell you to stay by the wall?"

THE SECURITY GUARD CHIMES IN.

SECURITY GUARD:

"Oh, I know where he is. I saw the group coming from around the corner earlier when I was coming to my post. There is an automatic sensor door at the top of the steps. Someone accidentally got locked out there last week while trying to get to terminal A. I bet you that's where he is. Let's GO get him."

▊ FLYY:

| "Don't move! We're coming to get you!"

▊ RIBBIT:

| "Okay!"

▊ NARRATOR:

"Flyy keeps on her Face Watch to keep an eye on her brother while they go get him. In a short time, RBT is rescued. Flyy warmly hugs her little brother, as she knows that she would have been in big trouble with her Mom."

Vocabulary Word: _____

The vocabulary word is **KIND**. Describe in your own words a time that you were kind to someone.

CHAPTER – 06

THE ADVENTURE

NARRATOR:

"It took them two minutes to rescue RBT. Meanwhile, Mom is so comfortable reading her favorite magazine that she forgets about the boarding time and that the children are gone for longer than expected. Dad, on the other hand, doesn't forget. He calls Mom. Mom's Face Watch beeps for a video call."

MOM:

"Hello?"

DAD:

"Hey, darling. Did the children check-in already with the Gate Agent?"

NARRATOR:

"Mom's eyes pop open. She becomes aware of the time and the announcements being made by the Gate Agent."

MOM:

"Oh, my gosh, oh, my gosh, the children! Ribbit! Flyy! O M G, Flyy was su- su-supposed to take him to the bathroom, and they are not back yet. Oh, my gosh! They are going to miss their flight!"

DAD:

"Calm down, darling. I'm sure they will be back on time."

THE GATE AGENT CHIMES IN.

GATE AGENT:

"Group 9 passengers are welcome to board Flight 9 0 0 1 to Miami through the main boarding lane."

DAD:

"Did he just say Group 9 passengers?"

MOM:

"Yesss!"

DAD:

"Oh, my gosh, oh, my gosh, where are they? Speak to the Gate Agent about holding the flight until they return."

MOM:

"I'll call you back!"

NARRATOR:

"Mom rushes to the podium next to the Gate Agent."

MOM:

"Hi! My children went to the bathroom and they are not back yet. Can you hold the flight until they return?"

GATE AGENT:

"Unfortunately, I'm not able to do that. You still have a few minutes before the door closes."

MOM:

"But you just announced Group 9 passengers. They are the last group to go on the plane."

GATE AGENT:

"Yes, ma'am, but we still have a little time left over when the last group boards just in case someone is running late. So, you still have a few minutes. They are the unaccompanied minors, right?!"

■ **MOM:**

"Yes, they are."

■ **GATE AGENT:**

"Oh, my gosh! I've been calling and paging them over the overhead intercom."

■ **MOM:**

"I'm so sorry. I was reading the magazine --- oh, never mind! How much time do we have?"

■ **NARRATOR:**

"Though Mom wanted to reserve the front seat, she decided to move to a corner seat. She was enjoying reading the magazine so much that she didn't want any interruptions."

HE CHECKS THE COMPUTER'S BOARDING SCREEN.

■ **GATE AGENT:**

"We have six minutes left."

■ **MOM:**

"Six minutes?! I thought the flight leaves at 10:10?"

■ **GATE AGENT:**

"Yes ma'am, it leaves at 10:10, but the computer preliminaries of the flight close out ten to fifteen minutes before the flight's door closes. We are at the sixteen minutes mark, which means we have six minutes left. At least five minutes now."

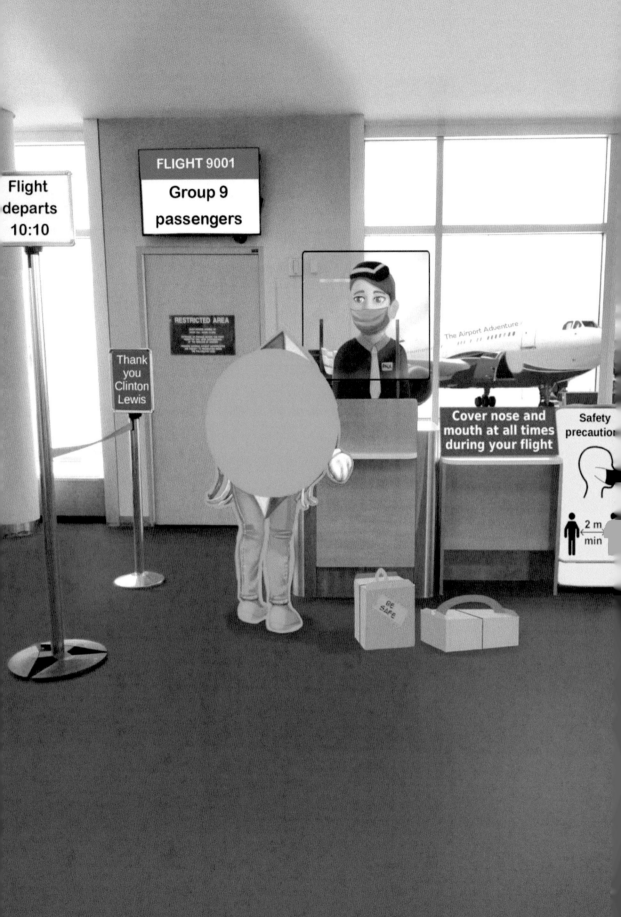

MOM:

"Oh, my goshhh! Ohhh, Face Watch!"

GATE AGENT:

"Face Watch? Excuse me?"

MOM:

"Nothing, not you!"

NARRATOR:

"Mom Face Watches Flyy, who is with the Security Guard and the Good Samaritan."

FLYY:

"Mom! I'm so glad you called. We just found Ribbit!"

MOM:

"Found Ribbit? What are you talking about?"

FLYY:

"I went to the bathroom and told him to wait outside and..."

MOM POLITELY CUTS HER OFF.

MOM:

"I don't mean to cut you off hon, but where are you?"

FLYY:

| "Upstairs."

MOM:

| "Upstairs?!"

FLYY:

| "Upstairs by the bathroom. Mom, I told you…"

MOM CUTS HER OFF AGAIN.

MOM:

"Hon, the boarding door closes in five minutes. You and your brother need to start heading this way. Hurryyyy!"

SECURITY GUARD CHIMES IN.

SECURITY GUARD:

"There is no way you guys are going to make it from here to there in five minutes."

MOM:

| "Oh, my gosh! Are you serious?!"

SECURITY GUARD:

"Yes ma'am! It's a good seven minutes walking distance from where we are to Gate F33. Six minutes tops if we hurry."

MOM:

"But the door closes in five minutes."

MOM TURNS TO THE GATE AGENT.

MOM:

"Are you sure you can't keep the doors open?! They will be here in six minutes."

GATE AGENT:

"I apologize for the inconvenience, but we have to close the flight out on time. I made four announcements calling for them. We have four minutes now. I have already checked the other flights, and we can get you rebooked on the next flight, which leaves in an hour."

MOM:

"Do you have a manager I can speak with?!"

SECURITY GUARD CHIMES IN AGAIN.

SECURITY GUARD:

"Oh, wait! I can call for Prospect to get us an electronic cart ride! Hold on a minute."

MOM:

"Hurry up, we don't have a minute to waste!"

SECURITY CALLS OVER HIS TWO-WAY WALKIE-TALKIE.

SECURITY GUARD:

"Prospect! We need an emergency ride from Gate F1 to Gate F33, ASAP!"

PROSPECT:

"Copy that! There is actually a cart close by dropping off someone at Gate F2. I will arrange for it to pick you up at F1."

SECURITY GUARD:

"Roger that! Let's GO."

NARRATOR:

"They run down the stairs and are just in time to meet the waiting driver. They jump onto the cart. The Driver knows the routine drill of trying to get passengers from one end of the terminal to the next."

DRIVER:

"Buckle up!"

GOOD SAMARITAN:

"Goodbye and be safe. Safe travels!"

THEY WAVE GOODBYE TO THE GOOD SAMARITAN.

NARRATOR:

"As they speed off, the tires make a shrill, squeaky noise. The Driver beeps his horn to move people out of the way. They are moving as fast as they can! "Hold ooonnnn…" says the Driver as he turns a corner. The cart is moving so fast that it tilts onto two wheels while going around the corner."

RIBBIT & FLYY:

"Wooooooo!"

DRIVER:

"Hold on tighter!"

NARRATOR:

"RBT, the security guard, and Flyy hold on as tight as possible. They make the turn safely and land back on all four wheels, but there is havoc in front of them. A passenger accidentally spilled a bottle of soda, and the cleaning maintenance person has cleaned it up to make sure no one slips and falls. It is a part of the airport safety protocol to safely place caution cones around the damp spot to block off usage until it is dry. It means there is only enough room for walking passengers or other staff to pass, but not a cart. The Driver beeps to get a maintenance person to come and safely move the cones for the cart to pass by, but there is no maintenance person.

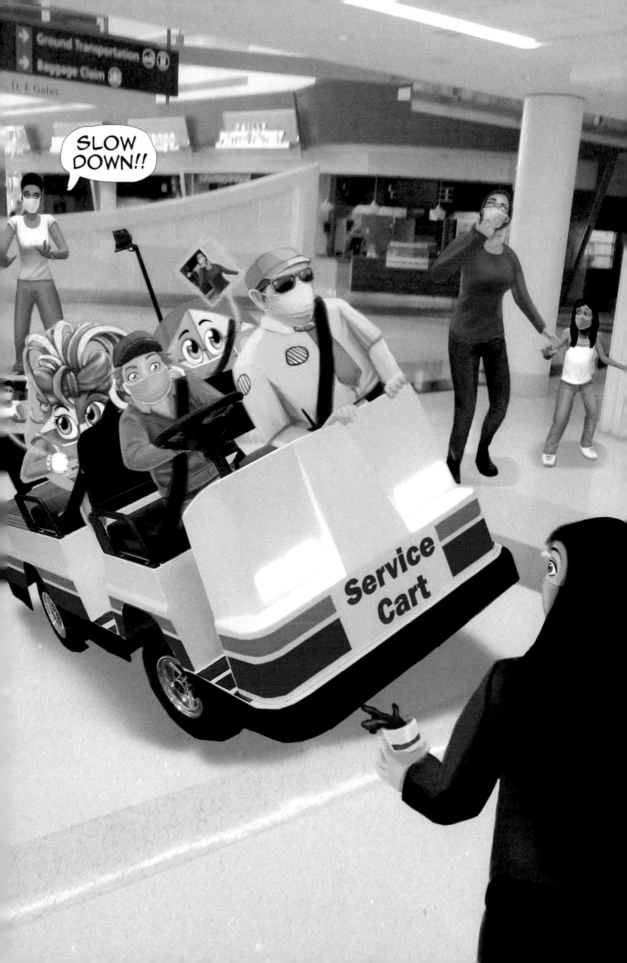

Two minutes and 30 seconds to GO! The Security Guard jumps off the cart, rushes over, and safely moves one of the cones. The Driver drives past the spill slowly to keep the cart from turning over. After they move a safe distance beyond the cones, the Security Guard returns the cone and jumps back onto the cart.

Did you catch that **SAFETY INFO ALERT**? There was no cleaning maintenance crew to remove the cones, so the person who was more qualified to move the cones did so in a safe manner. In times of emergency, look for the **INDIVIDUAL** who is more qualified to take over the emergency. The Security Guard makes it safely back onto the cart."

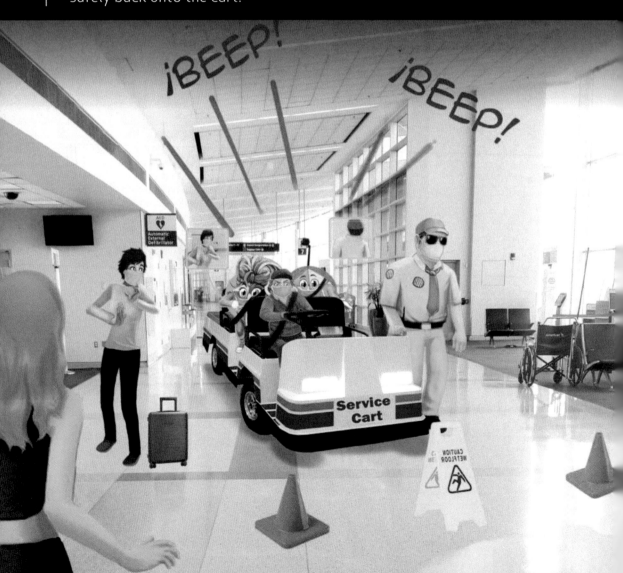

SECURITY GUARD:

"Full speed ahead. Let's GO!"

NARRATOR:

"The Driver speeds along, beeping furiously so no one will get in his way and passengers standing in the hallway jump out of the way to avoid being hit by the cart. As you can guess, this is not a safe thing to do. It is a **SAFETY INFO ALERT**. Speeding through the airport is an unsafe thing to do, even in the case of an emergency. Meanwhile, Mom is looking at her watch and counting down nervously.

The Gate Agent is patiently tapping his pen on the podium. Everything moves like a slow-motion scene in a movie, but in reality, the time is ticking away. One minute to GO and no RBT or Flyy! Forty-five seconds and still no RBT or Flyy. Then, at the thirty seconds mark, the cart comes speeding like it is in a NASCAR race. Mom jumps for joy and cheers the cart on. The gate agent looks up and sees them, and even he starts to cheer."

GATE AGENT & MOM:

"Hurry! Hurry! Hurry!"

Vocabulary Word: _____

The vocabulary word is **INDIVIDUAL**. Share about a time you stood out as an individual.

CHAPTER – 07

C.Y.

THE GRAND FINALE

NARRATOR:

"Fifteen seconds to GO! Fourteen seconds! Thirteen! Twelve! Eleven! Ten! Yessss! They make it. They scan the passes with only ten seconds left before the clock reaches its ten-minute mark. Whewww! The Gate Agent closes out the computer preliminaries of the flight just in time before the ten minutes mark. He stretches his hand to give Mom a high five because he is happy that he does not have to do such a cruel thing of leaving them behind.

Mom blows kisses to wish RBT and Flyy a safe journey. The other concerned passengers at the next gate start to clap and applaud. Even the viewers online that are watching on live stream are clapping as well. Mom is so happy she gives the gate agent a great big bear hug. He hesitates to return the hug because he knows everyone should be observing the COVID-19 social distancing precautions. Deep down he wants to return the hug, but he doesn't. He then closes the door. Even though he is in a hurry, he safely walks RBT and Flyy to meet the flight attendant that will attend to their flight needs. He hands the flight attendant the paperwork with the final passenger count and waits for it to be signed and returned by the captain and first officer.

Meanwhile, Mom happily thanks the Driver and Security Guard for their good deeds. While this is happening, the flight attendant placed RBT and Flyy in their respective seats, which are upfront and next to each other. Since Flyy is older, she has the window seat. RBT can still see outside when he leans over, which is what he is doing out of curiosity."

▌ RIBBIT:

"Who are those people with all those suitcases?"

▌ FLYY:

"They are the ramp agents. They are responsible for taking good care of the suitcases, other freight, and placing them on the aircraft."

▌ RIBBIT:

"Ok. Oh, oh, oh! What about that place over there? I remember seeing it when I was locked out. What is that?"

HE POINTS TO A BUILDING.

▌ FLYY:

"It looks like a tower on top of the airport. I think that's the Airport Tower."

▌ RIBBIT:

"What is an Airport Tower?"

▌ FLYY:

"I don't fully know. Hold on. Let me TEBIT it."

▌ RIBBIT:

"TEBIT it?"

▌ FLYY:

"Yeah, it's another word for learning more about something. It's like doing

your research on a project to learn more about it. So instead of saying, let me research it, I say, let me TEBIT it. It's a new generation thing. The older generation used the word research. We use TEBIT. Just like how some people use the word GOOGLE instead of search, as in GOOGLE it."

■ **RIBBIT:**

"Cooool. I like it. It also rhymes with my name Ribbit."

■ **FLYY:**

"Oh yeah, TEBIT, Ribbit. That's an excellent way to make a connection. I guess you will always remember it from now on."

■ **RIBBIT:**

"TEBIT."

HE LAUGHS OUT LOUD (LOL).

■ **NARRATOR:**

"Flyy presses and holds one of the buttons on her watch."

■ **FLYY:**

"Face Watch, what is an Airport Tower?"

THE WATCH RECITES THE DEFINITION.

■ **FACE WATCH:**

"An Airport Tower is where Air Traffic Controllers work. They provide ground-based air traffic directions for the aircraft on the ground and through the

airspace and can also provide advisory services to aircraft on the ground and through the airspace. They can also provide advisory services to the plane in non-controlled airspace."

RIBBIT:

"Wow! I didn't know that so many people worked behind the scenes to help us travel safely from one place to another."

FLYY:

"It is the same for our everyday lives. Remember, when Dad taught us that it takes a lot of people in our lives to help us grow up into our life's destination? The more you cut off or destroy those relationships, the less likely you will grow up safely into your destiny."

RIBBIT:

"You know what? I'm going to be best friends with everyone in the world so I can grow up and reach my life's destination safely."

FLYY:

"You can't be friends with everyone in the world, much less, best friends. That's impossible!"

RIBBIT:

"Why not? Remember, when Mom taught us about learning how to take something from one element and blend it into another element to make it work? So, I'm going to take what Mom taught us about what businesses do to get the most out of their best customers and then blend it into my quest to

get best friends. If the best business customers give the most, then my best friends shall do the same.

If I get everyone in the world to be my best friends, then I will get the most out of everyone. That's what best friends do anyway. They give more than regular friends. That's why customer service is so vital to every business. So, imagine if I provided the best friend service to everyone? They would become my best friends and give me the most. It is my theory of having best friends around the world instead of just regular friends, and I'm sticking to it."

◼ FLYY:

"Hmmm. You really have me thinking now. It makes a lot of sense. Again, that was another excellent way to blend the best customers in the business field with best friends in the social field! Plus, you would be like a superhero to the world if you are able to accomplish this."

◼ RIBBIT:

"I bet if you Googled it, it would show that no one has ever done it before. I can see myself being the superhero and being best friends with everyone in the whole world by providing the best friend service. I would be like my favorite superhero, Captain America: red, white, and blue. Plus, we are kites, remember that. We can do more things than humans can. Mom always says that."

◼ FLYY:

"You thought that out really well! I don't think anyone has ever done that before. You know what?"

◼ RIBBIT:

"What?"

■ **FLYY:**

"We are going to GO for it! I will be a **TEAM PLAYER** and help you become this superhero. When we get to our destination, we are going to TEBIT it and then GO for it! I almost forgot what Dad has always told us, 'If we see something, then say something.' Meaning, if we can see it in our vision and in our minds, then it's not impossible. It is possible, and we should say the words to help our vision come to life. It coincides with when Mom told us that if I want to be a pilot, then I must see myself as a pilot and then speak like a pilot because the pilot is already inside of me."

■ **RIBBIT:**

"Like this? This is Pilot Flyy; we're clear and ready to take off!"

■ **NARRATOR:**

"At that moment, the real pilot's voice comes on the intercom to announce the take-off process. They look at each other and laugh out loud. Did you catch that **SAFETY INFO ALERT** earlier? Mom and Dad's teaching coincide with each other. It allows the children to be safe in their thinking capacity. When parents say different things that do not coincide with each other, it brings confusion to the child's mind and makes him or her unsafe in their thinking and understanding."

■ **FLYY:**

"By the way, what Dad told us about our vision is almost similar to the airport's motto: 'If you see something, say something...'"

■ **FLYY & RIBBIT:**

"Hmmm!"

RIBBIT:

"Thanks for **ENCOURAGING** me to do this. It means a lot to me. Best Friends across the world! Now, really think about this. Having best friends gives me access to what my best friends have. In Spanish, they say, "Mi casa es su casa." So, imagine what I will have access to if everyone in the world is my best friend? I say, there are excellent benefits that come with having best friends rather than regular friends."

FLYY:

"Hmmm! Let's GO!"

NARRATOR:

"There is a **SAFETY INFO ALERT** on page 91. It is unsafe when you tell someone his or her dream is impossible. All things are possible to those who work accordingly to achieve it. Thank you for being a part of this adventure. It was a pleasure to have you! Hurray! To Be Continued…"

Vocabulary Words:

The vocabulary words are **TEAM PLAYER** and **ENCOURAGING**. Share with someone about a time you acted as a **TEAM PLAYER** and also as an

ENCOURAGER

ENCOURAGING (To self)

WELCOME TO THE
EDUCO BLEND

MAGAZINE

KITE
MANTRA
118

Personal
Safety
Tips
p.113

COVID-19
SAFETY
TIPS
106

AN
EXQUISITE
TASTE OF
THE AIRPORT
p.142

Live Safely
LV=55*

CONTENTS

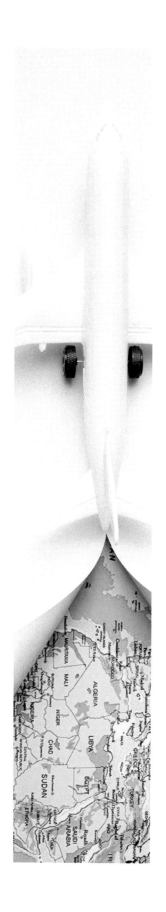

LiVe Safely

The word LiVe is uniquely spelled with the upper-case letters of L and V. When both letters are combined (LV) and translated into roman numerals, they equate to the number 55. On a weighing scale, the number 55 is the balance of one five on each side of the scale: equilibrium. Weight and Balance are necessary for an airplane to safely take off, go into flight mode, and safely land at a new destination. The Airport Adventure: LiVe Safely is about discovering how to balance one's life to Safely take off, transition, and Safely land at a New Destination.

The EducO Blend is a natural way to blend one or more entities in order to bring out greater points-of-view. The Airport Industry prioritizes safety and has a tremendous success rate in getting billions of passengers to their destinations; therefore, we will prioritize Safety in The EducO Blend to bring about different points-of-view. In doing so, we will use the terminologies, 'Aviation Thinking' or 'Aviated Thinking,' which is to apply the principles of the aviation industry to a different industry in order to bring out the best in that industry.

Safety: Noun

1. The condition of being protected from or unlikely to cause danger, risk, or injury.
2. The state of being safe and protected from danger and harm.

Aviation Thinking: ▶

The *decision-making* process of blending airport principles to safely take an idea, project, business, endeavor, individual, group, etc., to a higher altitude in order to land at a New Destination that is far above and beyond the original circumstance/location.

Example

A regular children's storybook to Book-A-Zine.

Aviated Thinking ▶

The natural flow and developmental growth of the mind that is on a higher level of operation and functionality.

Example

A person who uses Aviation Thinking as a natural way of life to socially grow and develop different levels of internal operations and external functionalities; an Aviator.

CO BLEND

News Articles

TEBIT the articles in this section.

1. *Aaliyah*

- https://www.biography.com/news/aaliyah-plane-crash-died
- https://en.wikipedia.org/wiki/Death_of_Aaliyah

2. *Kobe Bryant*

- https://www.cnn.com/2020/01/28/us/kobe-bryant-crash-timeline/index.html
- https://www.latimes.com/california/story/2020-02-02/kobe-bryant-faa-ntsb-safety

3. *Dr. Myles Munroe*

- http://www.tribune242.com/news/2015/feb/22/poor-decisions-crew-caused-myles-munroe-plane-cras/
- http://magneticmediatv.com/2015/02/final-report-on-myles-unroe-crash-released/

WHAT CAN FROM

While it is common for us to be remorseful of any tragedy that occurs in an unexpected and untimely manner, we can also be vigilant and learn from such circumstances. We must take time in the present moment to learn from past conditions so our future opportunities can be better decided. In other words, we must make decision-making progress, just as we make progress in other areas, like technology, daily living, eating habits, and so forth.

The three news articles mentioned previously describe three prominent individuals that were affected by the same element, which is the safety within the aviation industry. It is not by accident or favorable choice that safety is a priority in the aviation industry. The focus on safety is mandatory, and without such a pivotal element, the industry would not exist or would soon become extinct. A perfect example can be found in your own research of the financial impact of the airport industry (subdivision of the aviation industry) because passengers' safety was at risk during the 2020 pandemic. Safety can be considered the most

prized commodity on the face of the Earth. Without it, everything collapses.

All three news articles show the unsafe circumstances that led to the deaths of all three celebrities. Aaliyah's and Kobe's circumstances are a little different. Both celebrities ignored the aviation safety regulations that regular passengers would adhere to (or are subjected to), which resulted in their untimely deaths, along with the deaths of all the other passengers on board the aircraft or helicopter. In Aaliyah's case, a typical passenger would not have been able to load so many suitcases on a regular plane. In Kobe's case, ask yourself, would any regular passenger have been permitted to fly in such foggy unsafe weather, especially when other helicopters were grounded? In Dr. Monroe's case, the pilot had made an unsafe decision, and it resulted in the loss of lives for everyone that was on the aircraft, regardless of their status.

In the end, the three articles feature three lives and the lives of the other passengers that

WE LEARN THE PAST?

came to an untimely end. It is heartbreaking and mentally devastating to lose such valuable richness and pure assets, especially since they had a significant influence on the social well-being of so many people around the world. However, these are real stories, and we must learn from them. This way, we won't continue to make unsafe decisions that may cost us dearly financially, emotionally, physically, spiritually, socially, globally, and universally.

Safety is a commodity that must be taken into high consideration when it comes to human socialization. When a person is unsafe, he or she goes into survival mode, which warrants an automatic Fight, Flight, or Freeze mode. Once the person is in the survival mode, he or she may do something that causes the untimely destruction of a person, place, or thing. This same principle also applies whenever any equipment such as an aircraft or helicopter is placed in an unsafe circumstance. The circumstance may result in untimely destruction for those who are on board or in close proximity of such equipment, regardless of the person's celebrity status, wealth, health, title,

accomplishment, role, the goodness of his or her heart, etc.

We must learn that safety is a commodity that we cannot purchase. We can pay for security, but we cannot pay for safety. Safety is a universal law that governs everyone, everything, and every element accordingly without prejudice or favoritism. Those who violate it are bound to reap the repercussions. Safety must be a mandatory priority. We cannot pay for it. We cannot afford it. We cannot go around it. We cannot violate it. We must learn how to abide by it accordingly so that we can live longer than our current life expectancy.

This section is going to be a little tricky and unexpected but follow along and see if you are able to understand and learn something from it. Let us blend a vacation and job scenario as examples, so you can understand the safety decision-making process better: Once a person decides to go on a vacation, the person immediately begins to prepare for such vacation, even if the vacation is weeks, months, or even years away. By the time the vacation arrives, the person has typically already made all the necessary preparations. But believe it or not, the moment the person decided to go on vacation is the actual moment when the person began to take the vacation.

Let's say a woman is going on vacation and decides to lose fifty pounds before it's time to go. She immediately goes on a diet. Or she goes to the gym or begins to make mental preparation in how she is going to lose fifty pounds. This means she begins to live in the vacation mode the moment she makes her decision to go on vacation, even though she is not physically there (on vacation) yet. Some of her conversations will now include her telling others that she is going on vacation. She will begin to shop for vacation attire. She will plan what she will do while on her vacation. She will be so excited about her vacation that she may even start packing. Hence, her thinking and frame of mind are already on vacation, even though she is not yet on vacation. All of this happens because she made the decision to go on her vacation. In essence, once a decision is made, the tangible results take time to manifest into reality, as the decision pulls you closer to reality.

You can call the decision-making process 'the pusher.' The moment you make a decision, the process pushes you closer to reality, even if you are not consciously aware of it. Try it for yourself. Use the decision to go to the store as an example.

Now, let's look at a job scenario. Let's say that a male is hired during his interview and is told he will start the job the following month. But when does he 'get' the job? Is it the day he is hired, or is it the day he actually starts working? The answer is that he gets the job the day he is hired; however, he does not start the job until the following month. Once the

decision was made to hire him, that is the moment he got the job, even though he will not physically start until the following month.

Now, just like the vacation or the first day on the job, when we make an unsafe decision or a safe decision, we begin to live in that decision until the result(s) show up. Therefore, we must understand that the safe or unsafe decisions we make occur before the tangible results show up. It is quite scary to think that what happened to Aaliyah or Kobe began when the unsafe decisions were made to overload the aircraft or to fly in foggy weather. The results of each of these decisions were just waiting for the moment to show up. The unfortunate thing about this is that it is not only applicable to these two individuals, it is how the human mind works. Our thinking and decision-making process brings forth the tangible results in our lives, which automatically comes after the thinking is done or the decision is made. Some results show up immediately, some show up in days, and some show up in weeks, months, years, or even decades. So, this is something we can learn from. We must learn how to make safe decisions, or how to create the thinking pattern of the tangible results we desire to have one day.

Unfortunately, we live in a society that did not instill these vital life lessons in our childhood academic pursuits. Still, these lessons are nothing new; they have been around for centuries. They have been hidden from the masses but known by the elites. Just think about the saying, "As a man thinketh in his heart, so is he." (Proverbs 23:7.) This saying explains that what a person thinks within, so

> **"Our life is what our thoughts make it."**
>
> *Roman Emperor Marcus Aurelius*

> **"A man is what he thinks about all day long."**
>
> *Ralph Waldo Emerson*

> **"Do not think that what your thoughts dwell upon is no matter. Your thoughts are making you."**
>
> *Bishop Edward Steere*

will the person be in life, or outside (tangible). It also shows that there is some form of understanding about the thinking process in order for someone to have created such a saying. No one just comes up with such a powerful saying without having an in-depth knowledge or understanding of the topic. In reality it is not just a saying, it is a proverb from the bible: Proverbs 23:7. The bible is a book that has been around for over two thousand years. Again, this is nothing new, but it is just hidden from the masses. Our thoughts and our ability to think are more powerful than we have encountered within our elementary, middle, and high school academic knowledge. The intangible thought into the thinking process produces a tangible reality.

Here are some other prominent quotes pertaining to thinking:

I would like to recognize this poem as a tribute to these three lost lives and the lives of others in similar circumstances. It is the masterpiece poem by Maya Angelou, *"When Great Trees Fall."* You can Google her work and read such a beautiful masterpiece.

UPGRADE: COVID-19 PRECAUTION

School and Other Public Safety Tips

THE SAFETY VOWELS

PANDEMIC
SAFETY
TIPS

A *is for* **ATTENTION**

Pay attention to your safety and the safety of others around you.

E *is for* **ENCOURAGER**

Be an encourager to yourself and to others around you.

I *is for* **INDIVIDUAL**

Be your own person; be the person that you feel comfortable with, and in return, allow others to do the same.

O *is for* **ORDER**

Keep things in order for yourself and extend the favor if you can do it for others.

U *is for* **UNDERSTANDING**

Be understanding of your own value or potential value and the value and potential value of others around you.

is for Attention:

Pay attention to your safety and the safety of others around you.

Be compliant to the CDC rules, including six feet of social distancing, wearing your mask/covering effectively, washing your hands properly for 20 seconds, sanitizing areas that can be infected, and being compassionate about the well-being of yourself and others in your environment.

Washing hands:

Pre-wash your hands with clear, clean water for five seconds. This helps to break away or soften any negative participles on the hands. This is similar to washing dishes, washing laundry, or washing a vehicle.

The remaining 15 seconds of the required 20 seconds of washing should be spent adding soap (post-wash), then rinsing hands thoroughly. Lastly, apply a towel, cloth, air, or paper napkin to dry off hands.

Mask Wearing:

Safely lower your mask/covering every 45 minutes to an hour to get fresh air circulation.

It is important to wear your mask/covering, especially when in public spaces. Wear it because of the impact of COVID-19, and not just because your mother, father, friend, CDC professional, or teacher told you to do so. COVID-19 impacts the respiratory system, which includes the lungs and breathing organs (primarily the nose and mouth.) Wearing the mask/covering, especially in public spaces, lowers your chance of inhaling respiratory elements that are particles of the virus. These elements can be contracted through the sense of smell and are most effective when people are within six feet of each other. Hence, the requirement of wearing the mask/covering when in social settings. While we are not able to see these tiny particles with the naked eye, our sensory gland (smell) is able to detect them. The more microscopic COVID-19 particles we inhale, the more our respiratory system will be impacted. This, in turn, causes our respiratory system and sensory glands to shut down. The result is an untimely death.

**Please note that when we are in public buildings, the air is trapped within the building's parameters, which makes us more susceptible to inhaling these tiny particles. Wear a mask or face covering because you understand how respiratory viruses impact the body and how it is spread, and not just because someone required you to do so.

Remember

Safety starts with YOU. Try this experiment in your home: have a family member walk past you with a scented cologne or perfume and see how far away you are able to pick up the scent with your sense of smell.

Have you heard the expression 'Something smells fishy?' That 'fishiness' is the feeling of fear, and it impacts your reaction. In fact, it is the same process by which you can inhale the tiny particles of COVID-19, and it will indeed, impact your respiratory reactions. Our sensory ability to smell is a powerful process. Animals use such sensory smell to mate or select a partner, as do humans. Humans also use their scent of smell in other ways, namely deodorants, perfume, cologne, cooking, aromas, etc. This same process applies to infectious diseases or viruses. Hence, sanitizing also gets rid of the scented particles of COVID-19.

According to the World Health Organization (WHO,) the COVID-19 virus spreads primarily through droplets of saliva or discharge from the nose when an infected person coughs or sneezes, so it's important that you also practice respiratory etiquette (for example, by coughing into a flexed elbow.) This is one of the reasons that ventilating machines are necessary. They help the body regain its breathing functionality. Again, wear your mask/covering appropriately and effectively, especially when in public social settings. It is worth keeping you or others safe from the COVID-19. It is also worth keeping you off a ventilating machine.

Practice isolating yourself from others when you need to get a breath of fresh air. Go more than six feet away before lowering your mask/covering.

Care for your mask/covering when it is in your possession. Keep it clean and replace it if any damage has occurred. Examples of damage include loose strings, holes, torn fabric, dirt, not fitting tightly on your face, etc. The more effective the mask/covering is, the less likely you will be to inhale the tiny particles that make up COVID-19. This practice helps you to be attentive to your safety and the safety of others.

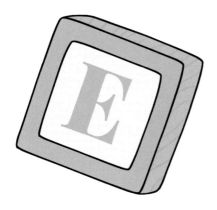

is for Encourager:

is for Individual:

Be an encourager to yourself and to others around you.

Use words that are kind and compassionate. Share with others who don't have what you have. Express your concern about their well-being. Send them a smiley emoji, encouraging text, video, picture, quote, etc. Encourage yourself and others to do the right thing in helping us to all be safe through this unprecedented pandemic. Encouraging yourself and others is a personal safety measure.

Be your own person; be the person that you feel comfortable with, and in return, allow others to do the same.

Wear the clothes that you can afford, and not just high priced name brands. Dress the way you prefer and resist wearing what others pressure you to wear. Speak in your true accent and not the way you think others want you to speak. Love the color you're in; appreciate what your life is, and not what you think it should be. Most of all, love the individual you are to the world. Knowing your individual worth through being your authentic self is a priceless safety commodity.

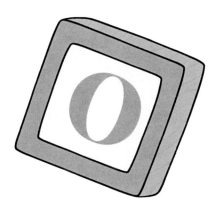

is for Order:

is for Understanding:

Keep things in order for yourself and extend the favor if you can do it for others.

Arrange your classroom neatly, which includes removing trash off the floor and sitting properly in your seat. Allow others to finish their sentence before you begin to speak, because speaking out of order causes a battle with others. Hand in your assignments on time. This creates a safe relationship between you and the teacher. Take turns going to the bathroom, remain in line when transitioning to class (if applicable), and wait for your lunch table to be called (if applicable) before attempting to get your lunch. Order is a form of placement safety; things that are in place in an orderly manner will remain safe.

Be understanding of your own value or potential value and the value and potential value of others around you.

What are you good at doing? What are you potentially good at doing? When you understand your own value, you can begin to use this value to enhance your life physically, emotionally, spiritually, socially, universally, etc. You can also share the same process with others. You should allow others to share their value with you as well. A 'shared value' classroom or home is a healthy, safe, and wealthy environment.

CYBER AND SAFETY

Internet Safety Tip:

Be careful how you share pictures or videos of your home and school environment online. Cyber stalkers who gain access to these pictures or videos can learn where everything is in your home or school, and this can make it easy for them to become physical thieves or burglars. If you share pictures or videos of you in different areas of your home, someone can collect those pictures or videos, create a collage, and then study the layout of your living environment.

This makes it easy for them to recognize what is in your house and where it is located. In turn, the thief or burglar who has a layout of your home will require less time to confiscate your valuable items from your home or school. If you must share pictures or videos, be consistent. Take your pictures or videos in one or two locations only.

The same applies to the school environment. If possible, remove all valuable items that will attract intruders. Although your online classes are offered on a secured platform, please use these precautions, as cyber intruders can hack any internet platform. Now that the 2020 pandemic has forced us to hold the majority of our engagements online, guess where most crimes will take place? Online! Practicing online safety is a personal choice of keeping your home or school environment safe from cyber or internet thieves and burglars.

Remember:

What you share online becomes public to everyone you allow to see it. This may not only harm your character, it can also influence how your family, friends, partner, and even strangers, view your overall character. Once you click 'send' your pictures and videos have the potential of becoming a public trend. We recommend 'double-thinking' about your decision before you click send/share.

INTERNET TIP

Essential Safety Checklist:

Before leaving your home, double-check your essential checklist:

- ➲ Keys (if applicable.)

- ➲ Mask/covering (check for discoloration as the mask wears out and becomes less effective.)

- ➲ Gloves (the gloves are especially handy if you have to assist a stranger in an emergency.)

- ➲ Sanitizers (wipes, spray, or gel.)

Personal Safety Tips:

Talk It Out:

It has been a long time since you last saw some of your friends and teachers in person. Naturally, your experiences have been different during the stay at home quarantine than they were when you were able to go to school. With this in mind, find a way to express your feelings and emotions about what you were going through during your time away from each other.

Be kind and have empathy toward each other:

You never know the residual effects someone may be experiencing after a trying event, especially an event like losing a family member or friend to COVID-19.

Be supportive and encouraging to each other, even if you are strangers:

This pandemic was an overwhelming surprise to almost everyone. You never know who is on their last breath.

Figure out how to make the school or classroom environment safe for everyone.

This includes bullying and harassment.

Remember this:

Seventy five percent of school shootings were done by students that were bullied or harassed.

Developmental Safety:

***Research (TEBIT) how to strengthen your immune system via google, books, or YouTube videos.

1. Allow yourself to make healthier choices in food, snacks, fruits, and vegetables.
2. Be active in the mobility of the body, which includes stretching your muscles.
3. Go online and learn about your chakras (key areas where the body stores energy) and how to cleanse them.
4. Allow at least eight hours of rest at night.
5. Decrease your stress levels by avoiding arguments, fights, disagreements, etc.
6. Minimize your differences with each other and improve your social interests.
7. Ask for help when things become too stressful or overwhelming, or when you simply don't know what to do.
8. Talk to someone when you don't feel safe in your environment, or when you feel uncertain about a decision.
9. Practice meditating, praying, chanting, mindfulness, yoga, or other rituals that can improve your cognitive existence.
10. Burn different incenses (sage, myrrh, frankincense, etc.) within a safe environment and allow them to help purify the air quality within your dwelling space.
11. Show appreciation and gratitude for yourself, your circumstances, and your loved ones.
12. **Spend time in natural environments (i.e., nature walk, by the river, by the beach, near streams, etc.)
13. Listen to sounds and rhythms that are therapeutic (YouTube has tons of videos.)

** Natural or unnatural environments contribute to and affect our well-being. What environment we spend most of our time in will determine what type of well-being we develop.

ENCOUR
SAFETY

The Elements of Encouragement (TEE)

Once upon a time, there were three encouraging elements to life. The first was a snake, the second was a hermit crab, and the third was a diamond. The snake (a reptile) has been known from the beginning of time. During its growth and development, it goes through a shedding process.

This process can be so painful when you think about your own human skin shedding, and the irritating pain it may cause. But the snake understands that in its developmental stage, it must shed the old skin, and inherit a new one. So, time after time, the snake sheds its old skin. Though it is painful, the process is needed for the snake to complete its growth and development.

The second was the hermit crab: a mighty small fellow with a jaw-dropping, grip-locking, heavyweight bite. While the hermit crab comes in a small package, it often requires a new shell to secure its growth and development. When it reaches a specific size in its growth (due to everyday nourishments) the hermit crab's body is no longer suitable to its once comfortable shell. Therefore, it must move from an uncomfortable shell to a more comfortable one because the place that usually gives it comfort can no longer provide such luxury. It is not an easy process to leave what was once comfortable and convenient to find something new, but for its developmental process to take place, the hermit crab has to move into a new shell.

Last, but not least, is the element of the diamond. Abundant in value, spectacular in its sight, the diamond lasts forever, and is known to be a girl's best friend. If you have someone that can help you walk through the harsh pressures of life and come out to be spectacular, the chances are high that the person would be your best friend. This is the history of diamonds which, by the way, are known to go through fiery pressure to obtain their diamond status, which lasts forever. So, no matter what pressure you are going through, a diamond knows such pressure

AGEMENT
SAMPLE

better than you, and it is the reason for its abundant value, a spectacular sight, longevity, and its best friend qualities.

No matter who you are, what position you are in, or what hard rocks you are between, be encouraged to know that the snake, the hermit crab, and the diamond are elements of encouragement. Through the pain, through the discomfort, through the pressures of life, these three elements have made it. If they made it, who are you, as a human being, not to make it also? You have such mighty power inside of you that can light up an entire country! Shed through the challenge like the snake, walk the discomfort like the hermit crab, and process the pressure like the diamond so that you can be of higher value, spectacular in the eyesight, and have a lasting and influential earthly testimony. The End!

The Kite Family

The characters of Book-A-Zine were carefully selected as the emphasis of a different form of aviation, something that is more practical and relevant to children than an aircraft. However, the characters' significance comes with their mantra, which helps them to be who they are. Their mantra is *"BE A KITE,"* which encourages them to fly higher above and beyond their circumstances. How are they able to do this? The word 'KITE' is broken down into an acronym.

THE

K KIND **I** INDIVIDUAL **T** TEAM-PLAYER **E** ENCOURAGER

MANTRA

K I T E

KIND
is for

KIND

Be Kind to others, which is to have a caring concern about the well-being of others.

Kindness is an act of human safety, which is why it was continuously repeated in the chapters of the story section.

INDIVIDUAL
is for

INDIVIDUAL

Be You. No other person can be like you.

Individuality is another act of human safety. Imagine how unsafe it would be for everyone to look the same, act the same, talk the same, dress the same, and be the same. So be YOU!.

TEAM-PLAYER
is for

TEAM-PLAYER

Be a Team player, which helps to lighten the load of the other members.

Team playing is an act of human safety. It takes the overwhelming weight off others.

ENCOURAGER
is for

ENCOURAGER

Be an Encourager: which is to support the growth and development of others.

Encouragement is an act of human safety. We sometimes fall off track and need to get back on track to continue the journey of life. Other times, we just need the extra strength of courage to face our challenges. Encouragement sweetens our moment to be optimistic.

Notice anything particular about the words used to form the *KITE* acronym? If you guessed that they are the vocabulary words in the story, you are correct. Understanding how to be *KIND* to others helps to generate a safe relationship. Being able to be your *INDIVIDUAL* self is a priceless commodity and a safe gem than being what others want you to be. Being what others want you to be results in you being an unnatural person who just lives up to someone's else's expectations. Being a *TEAM PLAYER* helps to safely distribute the load that the team carries in order to be victorious in the team's goal, vision, or mission. Being an *ENCOURAGER* for someone who doesn't see the need to move forward, is a life reward that is not measured in monetary payment. Therefore, to *"BE A KITE"* is to GO above and beyond your own self, as you are able to aviate others around you to go higher than their low survival mode. In return, it allows you to be the *KITE* you were created to be and to fly to a new destination...

BEST PRAC

TIPS

Here are five best practices to help improve our safety, universally and here on Earth. It takes practice and adjustment to become better at these safety tips. The more you practice them, the better opportunity you have to master them. Practice makes perfect.

1. Be Friendly With Others

The more enemies you have, the more unsafe you are as an *INDIVIDUAL*. People who are friendlier to others enjoy the benefits and comfort of being healthy. Being nasty, mean, disrespectful, inconsiderate, and selfish to others leads to stress factors in the body. In turn, this violates the body's safety mechanism (Fight, Flight, or Freeze mode,) which warrants untimely destruction of the internal organs and external expressions in a person's functionality. Being nasty, mean, disrespectful, selfish, or inconsiderate is not just displayed behaviors, each of these are signs that the internal safety mechanism has been violated, and these show up as survival expressions. Slavery was not or is not just a treatment; it was and is an unsafe

display of internal disturbance reflected in the outside functionality. In the end, those who were or are being enslaved face the external consequences of someone's internal disturbance.

In Summary:

Being friendly with others is a safety health component for one's life and functionality; it allows you to live your greatest possibilities in life. Learn how to be friendly and become healthy for your own life's functionality and the functionality of others. Be caring for others. Do something for someone without expecting anything in return. Be open to listening to others and hearing what matters to them. Share a safety tip with someone. Be a Good Samaritan to someone in distress. There are tons of ways to be friendly. Practice one of these ways, or practice many of them. The more you practice, the safer and healthier you become and the less likely you will be a candidate for COVID-19.

TICE SAFETY FOR SELF

2. Be Selfless

When you are in the process of flying on an airplane, there are safety announcements that are made before the aircraft takes off. One of the announcements is: *"If you are sitting next to someone who needs assistance, put on your mask first before assisting the person ..."* This announcement appears to say that you should cater to you before catering to someone else, but in reality, this is one of the most profound acts of selflessness that exists. The idea is that you cannot be of full use to anyone else if you are not fully safe and secured. Therefore, you are not just putting on your mask for yourself; you are preparing yourself to be fully available to help someone else. This is similar to wearing a mask for COVID-19 precautions. When you are not selfless, meaning you are selfish, you are not fully accessible to others. This means you are only partially functioning. To be partially functioning means that you are in an unsafe survival mode, which is the process of being selfish (not giving your all.) Hence, to be selfish is to be unsafe or (a 'dangerous good',) while to be selfless is to be safe and in full functionality.

3. Be a Pusher

As big and powerful as an aircraft is, it goes through a process called 'push back.' An airplane does not reverse like other vehicles; it must be pushed back in order for it to go onto the runway. As big and powerful as we are as human beings, we sometimes need a 'Pusher' in our lives. Sometimes we simply cannot see our way out of a circumstance and we need someone to help push us out of that circumstance. Ironically, these are often moments when a decision hasn't been made. This is the main reason why we call the decision-making process a 'pusher.'

For instance, many people believe they cannot rise above the circumstance in their community, family, or neighborhood. They do not *think they can achieve their dream.* They believe that "this is it," and this is all life is going to offer them. Being a Pusher is being the one who comes along and helps to break this cycle by pushing the person's mind to go above and beyond the circumstances: commit to a decision. That person who believes negatively may be a person who is capable of becoming an astronaut but settles on being a regular convenience store clerk. A Pusher would help to navigate this person toward the possibility of becoming an astronaut. Otherwise, the person may exhibit an unsafe mode of being unsatisfied with their partial potential, knowing that in reality, he or she desires to be an astronaut and not just a regular convenience store clerk.

> *NOTE:*
>
> *Being a Pusher is different from being a Supporter.* A supporter accepts whatever conditions the person has set for himself or herself, while a Pusher aviates the condition to go above and beyond the norm: particularly to commit to a higher level decision-making.

4. Be a Social Aviator

A typical Aviator is a pilot. A pilot is responsible for flying the aircraft safely at a higher altitude, far beyond the original location. If you are able to safely take a person, place, thing, or idea to a higher altitude beyond its original location using principles from the aviation industry, then you are considered an Aviator, but not one that is licensed by the state or government. Being a social Aviator is to be a pilot of your own circumstance, or the circumstance of others. It means that you can take an unfortunate circumstance and bring it to a whole new destination. In other words, you make it socially move from bad to good. In addition, you can take a good circumstance and move it toward a new destination to make it even better or safer. Therefore, as a social Aviator, you can safely take a good or bad circumstance and make it reach a new destination that is safe and healthy for everyone, not just some people. The world is calling for New Destinations!

As you probably know, we are not so safe in the world we are currently living in, even if the 2020 pandemic did not exist. Will you answer the call to be a social Aviator? It is a big focus for Aviated Thinking. Can you be the real-life superhero that makes someone's life safe? If you can do it for one person, you can multiply and do it for others.

5. Be a Newer

It is unsafe to do the same thing over and over again even if you are not expecting a new result. On the other hand, Einstein declared it insanity to do the same things over and over and expect a new result. So, whether you are expecting the same result or a new result, it is unsafe to do the same thing over and over again without including something new at some point.

Jobs allow workers to take a vacation for this same reason, mainly because it is safe to do something new every once in a while. Sometimes you must reinvent yourself and become safe again. An aircraft does not fly continuously; it lands, refuels, boards new passengers (and sometimes a new crew,) and starts a whole new trip. Even if the trip is to the same destination, the passengers, suitcases, food, etc., are all new. This is why you should be a Newer and add something new to your life every now and then. It helps to keep you safe and healthy, as old things tend to get spoiled, rotten, or outdated. One good example of being a Newer is the Phoenix bird, a bird that is known for its great strength and ability to renew itself.

By the way, did you know that the aviation industry based its foundation, growth, and development on the bird species? The word aviation is a blend of a word and a suffix, 'avi' and 'ation.' 'Avi' is the Latin word for a bird, and 'ation' is the suffix that means action or in progress. Having this understanding, the Newer became the aviation industry as airplanes, helicopters, kites, blimps, space shuttles, human gliders, and drones are now able to do the same actions that an Avi bird does. It all started from the concept of 'practice makes perfect.' Today, the aviation industry has perfected the craft of making airplanes and other flying contraptions fly like a bird.

Try eating something new.

Try going somewhere new.

Try doing something new.

Try thinking of something new.

Try cooking something new.

Try speaking to someone new.

Try watching something new.

Try reading something new.

Try wearing something new.

FROM HERE TO THERE

With the support and purchase of each T-shirt, you help to strengthen our mission to deliver SAFETY to a Global market and Beyond...

Cleous "Glowry" Young

THE TEB-IT
FOUNDATION

Cleous "GloWry" Young

Founder & President

The TEB-IT Foundation is the fundamental source that channels *The Airport Adventure*. Our mission is to provide Universal Safety for All, which is deeply rooted in our Philosophy, ***"One for ALL and all for ONE."***

If you would like to donate or contribute to our mission, please feel free to visit our website at www.thetebitfoundation.org or scan the QR code (Applicable on Smart devices) and it will take you there automatically. Thank you in advance for your generous support. Be Safe! Be Healthy! Build New Possibilities!

Yours Truly,
Cleous "GloWry" Young
Founder & President

Safety is Paramount!
LiVe Safely!

7 SIMPLE SAF
HUMAN SO

01

Ask when you don't know something, or when you are unsure what to do...

➲ It allows you to make more safe decisions.

Keep your environment and the Earth clean...

➲ It allows you to be safe in your travels and keeps your mind flowing, organized, and in order.

02

03

Find someone you can share your inner concerns or challenges with. Someone who will accept you, understand you, and respect your safety and security...

➲ It helps to keep your internal organs healthy and stress-free.

Practice resolving unresolved inner emotional challenges...

➲ It prevents the future build-up of emotional distress, psychological disorders, adult drama, and functionality limitations.

04

ETY TIPS FOR
CIALIZATION

05

Practice using words on yourself and others that increase value and worth...

➲ It allows you to grow and develop in a mature manner.

Practice getting enough sleep/rest before school, work, or athletic engagements...

➲ It allows you to function more effectively when doing any task.

06

07

Practice researching ('TEBI'ing) or studying a topic, and not just making assumptions...

➲ It allows you to be more trustworthy and increases your inner confidence.

Practice adhering to the Earth's, environment's, person's, or equipment's safety protocols. Also, never ever forget to adhere to the airport industry's safety protocols when flying, because it is worthy of such a practice. "If you see something, say something ..." is one of the elements within the airport safety protocols, and it is there for a reason.

BONUS

IMPROVING SOCIALIZA

Here are nine (9) elements in the Airport Industry that can help you improve your Human Socialization Skills once you are able to blend them into your life. You can use one or two of these elements, all nine, or any amount you wish. They are successful elements used in the Airport Industry and have already been proven to have credible outcomes. If you are looking for a credible outcome in a specific area, then you can use these to sharpen your skills. Remember, someone blended the bird industry to form the growth and development of the aviation industry. Then someone else blended the kite industry to form the airport industry. So, you can blend the airport industry to formulate your growth and development industry.

Learning Options and Their Translations:

The Translation Version is the process of translating a word or phrase from a different occupation to gain understanding in a new language or scenario. The context remains the same; however, the language is different.

YOUR HUMAN TION SKILLS

The nine (9) elements are:

Black Box

JetBridge

Luggage Tag

Weight and Balance

Boarding Pass/Ticket

Arrivals and Departures

Circling

Runway

Buddy Pass

1. Black Box:

A Black Box is a flight data recorder that stores information on specific parameters (such as flight control and engine performance) and a cockpit voice recorder, which records background sounds and conversations between crew members and air traffic control. When there is an accident, the Black Box is used to collect data of the *conversations* or *background sounds*. It is one of the safest pieces of equipment on the aircraft.

Translation:

Having someone that can be your Black Box in times of an accident (when you hit rock bottom) or when you face a challenge, can therapeutically work wonders for you. Your Black Box is someone who will be there to listen attentively without any form of judgment, criticism, or ridicule. Allowing you to share your innermost *pressing thoughts, sounds* (cry, sob, etc.), or concerns without interruption is a priceless commodity. You can call this process the Black Box Friendship (BBF) because the person becomes your Black Box Friend and allows you to share freely what is on your mind, especially when you are experiencing tough times. The person must be committed to keeping your shared information safe and secure, even if you pass away. It works wonders to the mind and body when that safe space is shared freely.

2. Weight and Balance:

Each aircraft goes through what is called a maximum take-off weight process. This is the maximum weight allowed on the aircraft in order for it to take off the ground safely and reach its destination. It includes the weight of the aircraft and its fuel, and the weight of the baggage, passengers, freight, and crew. When the balance is off during the flight, it can cause an extreme catastrophe for everyone and everything on board the aircraft.

Translation:

Your own life is impacted by the things you intake (fuel,) the things you carry physically or mentally on a daily basis (baggage), the people you hang around (passengers,) and the things you do (your crew.) They all take a toll on your life, and if you are not able to balance them accordingly, their weight will drag you down. Learn how to weigh and balance your life daily so that you are not overloaded or overwhelmed. Because if you are, this may cause a crash in your life. Weight and Balance are not just for an aircraft. People often use the words "burnt out" when their weight and balance is not in alignment. Learn how to weigh and balance your life by not overloading too many things. Anything that is too much in excess becomes overweight. This includes too much arguing, fighting, eating, working, talking, thinking, worrying, social media, etc.

3. Circling:

When, for whatever reason, an aircraft is not able to land, it flies around in a circular pattern. This holding pattern is due to some unsafe circumstance with the weather, in air traffic, or at the landing space at the airport terminal. During this circling process, the crew takes extra precautions to make a safe landing when the conditions are finally clear to do so.

4. JetBridge:

A JetBridge is an often enclosed, movable connector which most commonly extends from an airport terminal gate to the aircraft. It is what allows the passengers and crew to board or deplane the aircraft, and it helps protect passengers or crew members from going outside and being exposed to harsh weather.

Translation:

There are times that you need to take a step back and circle around on a decision-making process, especially when the outcome doesn't look safe. Often, people make quick decisions that aren't thoughtfully processed. They live to regret those decisions later on. Therefore, it is wise to have a circling moment at times, especially when the circumstance is difficult or unsafe. Don't just rush into a circumstance or situation because it looks good or feels good. Take some time to think about it. Be logical, mathematical, realistic, and futuristic. Also take note that an aircraft does not circle all day and all night, because if it did, it would run out of fuel or create a fatigue moment for passengers and crew which would make it unsafe. The same goes for your circumstance or situation. Don't take forever to circle with your decision-making process.

Translation:

The JetBridge is a connector that allows a connection to be made so that what is difficult becomes easy. There must be one or more Jetbridge connectors in your life that can be enabled for your difficult circumstances to become easier. Whether the connector is spiritual or physical, the connection must arrive with the outcome making something easier. The connector is often referred to as a GO TO person. Maybe it is a family member, a friend, a relationship person, a business partner, a teacher, a principal, the crossing guard, a security guard, an elder, or someone you can trust and feel safe sharing your information and space. Whoever it is, the connector is that GO TO personnel that can bridge things and make them easier and more reliable for you to cross into a new environment.

5. Boarding Pass:

A boarding pass is a document provided by airlines during the check-in process, which permits passengers to enter a specific restricted area of an airport, and then to board the aircraft for a particular flight. At a minimum, it identifies the passenger, the flight number, the date, and the scheduled time of departure.

Translation:

Do you have a life's pass that provides you with specific permission to board a particular restricted area? It is not a physical membership pass that gets you access to a club, but rather a specific talent, gift, skill, knowledge, or understanding. A specific talent, gift, skill, knowledge, or understanding are all life passes that allow you to get access to restricted areas in your life. At a minimum, this life's pass helps identify who you are, what type of pass you have, what you are able to do with the pass, and how others can benefit from it. Every person has their own life pass, and every person must discover it for themselves. You must discover this pass so you can board your life to a New Destination. Your ticket was purchased for you to be born, but you have to discover your life's pass in order to get to your destination. This experience has a quality that allows you to gain a new friend, a new relationship, a new opportunity, a new possibility, a new career, a new award, a new promotion, a new destination, etc.; a quality that gives you access to board a restricted space that others may not have access to. Otherwise, you will lack the access of a quality life and settle for the bare minimum of what is handed out to you. Your talent, gift, skill, knowledge, or understanding is your boarding pass to a greater quality of life for yourself and also for your friends and family. You must discover it!

6. Runway:

This is the long or short rectangular space provided on land from which the aircraft can take off or land. Without this designated space, the aircraft is not able to safely take off or land.

Translation:

As powerful as an aircraft is, without the proper amount of space to take off or land, it would lose the power and functionality to go up into the air and come down to the ground. The same goes for people. People need a safe space to develop mental maturity and grow into a more adult-like body. More specifically, you need your private and public spaces, because they allow you to be you. Your own runway space will enable you to flow, grow, develop, and function in the manner in which you were created. Some people refer to this by saying, "I need my space," or, "I need some space." The latter typically relates to issues within a relationship. It is the runway space that allows flow, growth, development, and functionality that the person is referring to. Hence, the space/runway allows a powerful functionality to take place, whether it is entering into the space or leaving the space. The term 'social distancing' is now widely used to relate to such a needed space. However, space (runway) is an innate daily operation of one's life in order to help you flow, grow, develop, and function effectively.

---

7. Luggage Tag:

A luggage tag (also known as a bag tag) is used to identify a person's luggage when it arrives at its final destination. While many luggage pieces may appear to have the same design and colors, the tag helps to separate and identify each piece of luggage. At a minimum, the tag includes the person's name, email address, and phone number.

8. Arrivals and Departures:

Arrivals and Departures are terms used by the airport to identify inbound flights (arrivals) and outbound flights (departures). By using these terms, the airport staff knows precisely what flights are coming in and going out, which helps to create the cultural experience of the airport. If airport passengers do not know any other airport terms, they certainly know 'arrivals' and 'departures.'

Translation:

What identifies you to be an INDIVIDUAL when you are among others who are the same? Sometimes a person gets lost into being a stereotype. Even worse, sometimes people are victims of mistaken identity. These situations can be unsafe and costly for that person. Therefore, having a tag that distinguishes you from others helps to break away from being stereotyped or being caught up in a mistaken identity. Here are some things that tag you: your hair, attire, smell, attitude, word usage, name, complexion, demeanor, your friends and associates, your reputation, your facial expression, your integrity, and your humor.

Translation:

Arrivals and Departures are also terms that are used in the human socialization field. They signify what things are 'arriving' inside of you, (i.e.: food, thoughts, sights, sounds, smells, tastes, touch, etc.) The arrivals create the culture of who you are. In terms of 'outbound' or 'departures,' these describe what things are coming out of you (i.e., your words, attitude, attire, etc.) These things help to identify the culture of who you are to the world. The inbound and outbound of who you are help to create the cultural experience of what you are to yourself and to others, which significantly impacts and influences your life's destination. If others consider you a threat, or dangerous goods, then more than likely, they will not want to be around you. On the other hand, if they think you are safe or suitable to be around, then more than likely they will want to be around you and often will want to help you succeed.

9. Buddy Pass:

A Buddy Pass is a non-revenue, standby ticket provided as a benefit to all airline employees. The employees share the pass with friends and family so they can enjoy some of the airline's benefits, even though they don't work for the airline company. In this case, it is a similar blended context of the phrase, "Mi casa es su casa," which means "My home is your home."

> *Translation:*
>
> Not everyone will be employed with the same company or have the same talents, knowledge, understanding, skill, or gift as you. Therefore, how can the things you benefit from in your own life benefit your friends and family so that they are able to call you a buddy? A truly selfless act is to use your own life's benefits to benefit the lives of others around you. Sometimes individuals around you are not able to accomplish specific goals, dreams, or visions. Rather than disregarding their ability, you can look at how your own accomplishments can benefit them as well. Again, this concept is captured in the Spanish saying mentioned above, "Mi casa es su casa," which is translated as, "My home is your home." The same can be blended as "My benefits are your benefits." Imagine this: if the author of this book were selfish, you wouldn't know about this story or magazine information. Be a buddy to others and pass on your benefits so they can benefit as well. It is an overall safe and kind act to do.

SAFETY:

Safety is the number one priority in the Airport
Industry. Safety plays a pivotal role in our lives
as well. For example, are we safe around our
friends, family, neighbors, co-workers, and
classmates? Does it cost you mental anguish the
same way it costs the airport industry financial
liabilities when there is an unsafe circumstance?
Just as safety affects the airport industry, it also
affects our everyday lives. The body's modality
operates in safety, and when it feels some form
of threat or danger, it goes into a Fight, Flight,
or Freeze mode. Hence, SAFETY is the number
one priority of the human body. It can impact us
spiritually, emotionally, physically, psychologically,
universally, and socially when there is an unsafe
environment or circumstance that is presented to
us. It must be mandatory for human socialization
to go to a New Destination where safety is the
newly used commodity. Otherwise, we will
continue to perish in survival mode, and in that
case, we are not living our life's best and fullest
potential. Just look at the number one request
in the 2020 pandemic, which is to be SAFE from
COVID-19. Hence, you need to add the space,
language, culture, or environment for safety in your
individual way of life or lifestyle, as safety starts
with YOU. Then watch as the remarkable happens.

DID YOU

An Air Hostess is now called a Flight Attendant, and the word 'airplane' is now being interchanged with the word Aircraft (as has been purposely done in the story portion of this book.) As the industry progresses, some of the terminologies have transitioned to fit the industry's new progression. The same transition must happen in the human socialization field. Progress requires something of the past to be adjusted in order to fit the present. Safety has been a priority from the beginning of the Airport Industry, beginning with the Wright Brothers in 1903. It is time for the past (Airport's priority) to be applied to the present (Human Socialization,) as safety is not just for the airport industry's daily operation, it is a necessary commodity for the flow, growth, development, and functionality of our humanity that requires spiritual, physical, social, emotional, psychological, and universal progress.

While the Aviation Industry saw its model developed from the context of the Avi bird, the airport industry (a subdivision of the aviation industry,) saw its development from the study of the kite. Did you know that many greats, including the Wright Brothers, studied the element of the kite to help distinguish the development of some essential elements that are in use in today's society?

According to the American Kitefliers Association, men like Benjamin Franklin and Alexander Wilson applied their knowledge of kite flying to gain a better understanding of elements such as electricity and lightening (The Kite Experiment.) Sir George Cayley, Samuel Langley, Lawrence Hargrave, Wright Brothers, and Alexander Graham Bell all experimented with the kite and contributed to the evolution of the airplane. The U.S Weather Bureau flew kites to raise meteorological instruments, which contributed toward knowing the weather forecast. The military once used the kite to gain a better understanding of their opponent's distance along with using the kite as human transportation. The Micronesian people used the kite for fishing. The kite was also used as a messaging element from one person to another. The kite was an essential element used to develop some of today's industry. Imagine what the kite can be used for today!

KNOW?

Bonus:

Did you know that it is unsafe to fly a commercial passenger aircraft with just one pilot? A second pilot is needed in case something goes wrong with the first pilot. The first pilot is called the Captain (wears four stripes on the uniform,) and the second is called the First Officer (wears three stripes on the uniform.) The First Officer is second-in-command of the aircraft, similar to a vice-president being second-in-command to a president. The First Officer also plays the role of a *Kind Team Player* that helps and encourages the Captain, as well as takes some of the load off the Captain.

Translation:

It should be mandated unsafe to have only one teacher in a classroom of students. Each classroom should have a teacher's assistant to help facilitate the lesson or answer individual concerns for those students who are not able to keep up with the lesson. Though having a lone teacher is done quite frequently in some classrooms, it is unsafe for the overall functionality of the students' growth and development. Being the lone teacher in a classroom carries the same blended weight and balance (and responsibility) of a single-parent home versus a two-parent home. It is unfair for teachers, and it is unsafe for the students; but overall, it is unsafe for the growth and development of the student population. The assistant is a *KITE* member that should take some of the load off the teacher and students and thus make the classroom learning environment fully safe so it can run smoothly.

Did You Know?

Safety Matters:
it is the root / foundation / nucleus of your greatest possibilities.

"WE CAN ATTEMPT TO BUILD OR BUY ALL THE SECURITY MEASURES AND ATTEMPT TO KEEP US SAFE FROM EACH OTHER, OR WE CAN PRACTICE HOW TO LIVE SAFELY WITH EACH OTHER AND AVOID THE HARSH REALITIES OF HURT PEOPLE HURT PEOPLE.

CLEOUS "GLOWRY" YOUNG

THE RECIPE OF THE AIRPORT ADVENTURE

AN EXQUISITE TASTE OF THE AIRPORT

INGREDIENTS

1. Air .... 33 gallons of above and beyond AIR

2. Benevolent .... 1 ounce of requested Benevolence

3. Brilliancy .... 1 pint of demanded Brilliancy

4. Creativity .... 1 pint of Creativity

5. Determination .... 1 teaspoon of Determination

6. Divinity .... 1 gallon of Almighty Divinity

7. Dream .... 1 ounce of a night's Dream

8. Encouragement .... 2 pounds of Encouragements

9. Exquisite .... 1 ounce of Exquisiteness

10. Flavor .... 1 tablespoon of Favor

11. Fun .... 1 gallon of authentic Fun

12. Healing .... 12 pints of Healing

13. Innovative .... 1 teaspoon of Innovation

14. Knowledge .... 3 quarts of Knowledge

15. Love .... 7 pints of Love

IN THE MEMORY OF MY BROTHER CHEF MIC<u>HEAL</u> YOUNG 01/13/2021.

"May your life be <u>healed</u> in a Higher Destination"

INGREDIENTS

16. Meditation.. 1 quart of nightly Mediations

17. Patience .... 10 pounds of Patience

18. Persistent.. 2 tablespoons of Persistency

19. Prayer .... 1 quart of steadily Prayer

20. Safety.. 1 gallon of prioritized Safety

21. Sage .... 1/4 cup of Sage

22. Sauce .... 1 cup of secret Sauce

23. Seasoning... 2 pounds amplitude of Seasoning

24. Standards.. 3 pints of Standards

25. Support.. 1 ounce of outside Support

26. Timing.. 10 grams of Timing

27. Universe.. 1 gallon of Universal Connection

28. Understanding .... 3 quarts of Understanding

29. Value .... 18 gallons of Value

30. Wisdom .... 3 quarts of Wisdom

Marinating:

Seasoning:

The Airport Adventure (TAA) was first written under the name 'FliFo and RGT are on the GO' within the last quarter of year 2018-19. Inside the story, you will constantly see the word 'GO' in uppercase letters, which is a part of keeping the original context of the story. The story was originally written with specific airport terminologies for the target audience of the airport industry. It was later translated into layman's terms for the understanding of non-essential readers that are not part of the airport industry. At that point, the name was converted into *The Airport Adventure*. It marinated in storage for over 12 months before being considered for publication. This consideration was triggered by the death of Kobe Bryant on January 26th, 2020.

The Airport Adventure is seasoned down to the backbone of every page. With an exquisite offer, readers are able to gather a taste of creativity, innovation, possibility, golden opportunity, and authenticity, which is served with the sauce of brilliancy. In today's time, we desire for our readers and consumers of the product to be brilliant. Therefore, we added a special VALUE sauce of brilliancy to go with each reader as they consume the product. We anticipate for this first series to whet your appetite of coming back for more in the upcoming series of *The Airport Adventure*. Please dine safely and responsible.

Prepared:

Serving:

The Airport Adventure was prepared and cooked with the intentional thoughts of the universal energy of safety, love, care, togetherness, team, fun, family, friendship, healing, victory, possibility, joy, anointing, value, life, understanding, wisdom, knowledge, contribution, and pride in such brilliant quality. Hence, you are able to taste an exquisite part of the Airport you have never tasted before!

The Airport Adventure is served with the utmost respect and appreciated-value to its readers and consumers. Without readers and consumers, there would be no reason to create such a product. Hence, we purposely fill each serving with the finest and purest gratitude and appreciation found on earth for our readers and consumers. We thank you in advance for accepting such serving. Namaste!

Taste:

We envision creating a taste-bud worthy product tender enough to offer a mouth-watering super-duper exquisite *TASTE* of the Airport Industry for the entire world; an exquisite caliber of taste never offered to the world before.

LiVe Safely!

**

The word *LiVe* is uniquely spelled with the upper-case letters of *L* and *V*. When both letters are combined (*LV*) and translated into roman numerals, they equate to the number 55. On a weighing scale, the number 55 is the balance of one five on each side of the scale: equilibrium. Weight and Balance are necessary for an airplane to safely take off, go into flight mode, and safely land at a new destination. The Airport Adventure: *LiVe* Safely is about discovering how to balance one's life to Safely take off, transition, and Safely land at a New Destination.

Made in the USA
Middletown, DE
04 June 2021